LAKESHARK!
INVASION OF THE ASIAN CARP

Alan D. Roebuck

Tortoise Shell Publishing Company | Ann Arbor, Michigan

Copyright 2014 by Alan D. Roebuck

All rights reserved under International and Pan-American Copyright Conventions. Published in the United States by Tortoise Shell Publishing Company, Ann Arbor, Michigan. 48103.

No part of this book may be reproduced, scanned, or distributed in any printed or electronic form without permission. Please do not participate in or encourage piracy of copyrighted materials in violation of the author's rights. Purchase only authorized editions.

Tortoise Shell Publishing Company is a Michigan Corporation.

Library of Congress Cataloging-in-Publication Data:

Roebuck, Alan D.

"Lakeshark!"

"Invasion of the Asian Carp" Subtitle.

Library of Congress control number: 1-1282410091

ISBN 10: 0990336301

ISBN 13: 978-0-9903363-0-3

   1. Fiction.   2. Asian Carp   3. Environmental   4. Cautionary tale.

Cover design by Steven Lomas

Text formatting by Jon Roty. Lily Pad Graphics

Printed by Cushing-Malloy. Ann Arbor, Michigan.

Naturally printed in the United States of America.

This book is a work of fiction. All characters are born from the author's imagination.

Permission to excerpt passages from the book will often be granted with written permission from the author. All rights reserved. All motion picture rights are held by the author.

Bulk purchases for educational purposes are offered at a substantial discount.

To order, please contact www.tortoiseshellpublishingcompany.com.

— *Dedication* —

To my wife, Cyrene.
It's not easy being married to a writer.

Special thanks
to
Tim Foley
and
Wendy Frisch
for their proofreading skills.

— *Contents* —

One.	Meet Emily and Lisa	9
Two.	The Chicago Barriers	13
Three.	The Lecture	23
Four.	The Big Rain	29
Five.	The Fish Kill	37
Six.	Two Years Later	41
Seven.	The Metamorphosis	47
Eight.	Going to Grand Haven	51
Nine.	The Grand River	59
Ten.	Rough Day On Beaver Island	67
Eleven.	Officer McFadden	83
Twelve.	Back in Grand Haven	99
Thirteen.	The Cigarette Hull Boat Trip	107
Fourteen.	The Recovery Mission	133
Fifteen.	Searching North Fox Island	149
Sixteen.	Preparing to Display the Fish	161
Seventeen.	The Media Event	169
Eighteen.	The Coroner	179
Nineteen.	Making Arrangements	183
Twenty.	Wrapping Things Up	185

— Prelude —

This story is a work of fiction but the basis for it is very true. Four species of Asian Carp are close to entering Lake Michigan through the Chicago waterways. They have changed the ecosystem in the Mississippi River and in its connecting waters. Altering the food chain from the bottom up, Asian Carp have devoured most of the small organisms as well as eliminating the food source other organisms needed to survive; everything has changed.

In many of those rivers and connecting lakes, the physical amount of living organisms, called "biomass," has shifted from 0% Asian Carp to over 98% Asian Carp within just a few years. To say they have taken over is an understatement.

The locations in the story—Chicago, Grand Haven, and Beaver Island—are all intended to be accurately depicted. The biology in the story is accurate.

Written so that anybody can read it, perhaps it will inspire a young reader to take up the field of biology. For everybody else, if the story encourages people to be more environmentally conscious, then it has served an important purpose.

It is a story about change.

Alan D. Roebuck

2014

Chicago Area Waterway System

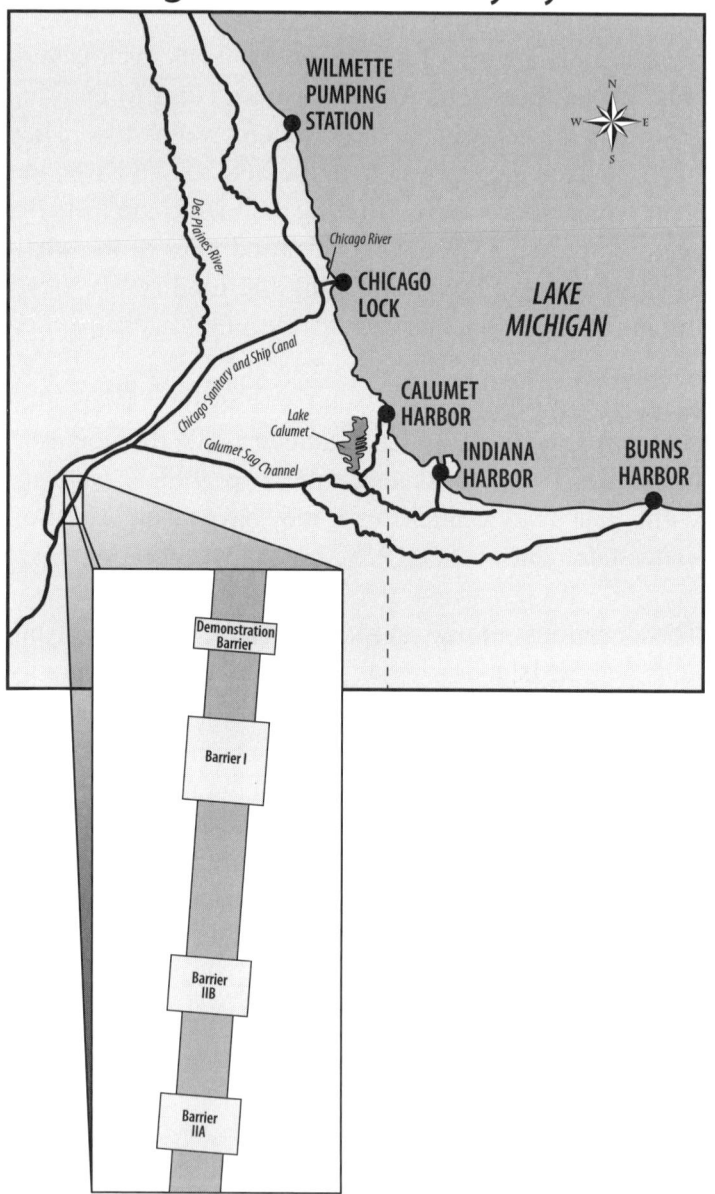

Inset: Electric barriers designed for fish deterrence

CHAPTER ONE
MEET LISA AND EMILY

Knee deep in the Lower Chicago Sanitary and Shipping Canal, Lisa bottled up another sample of water. Recently graduated from the University of Florida, this was her dream job. Not only was she doing what she loved to do, she was working with Emily. They were new friends, having been hired by the Shedd Aquarium in Chicago within months of each other. Both 25, they hit it off immediately: not only did they have identical interests, they both liked to work hard. And party hard.

They were tracking the migration of Asian Carp—the invasive species threatening to enter the Great Lakes. Both Lisa and Emily had graduated from college with master's degrees in Marine Science. Lisa Brown studied jellyfish down in Florida. She chose this phylum, the Cnidarian Phylum, because she liked the fact that they could fend for themselves. Of course, she had been stung numerous times, so much she felt she may be becoming immune to the poison. She had also been hurt in a relationship years ago and would rather be stung by an unthinking jellyfish than by a person who should have known damage was being inflicted.

Emily French studied at Boston University. Impressed that sturgeon have existed for over one hundred and fifty million years, she wrote her master's thesis on the sturgeon's ability to survive in a very different ecosystem than the one in which it began. This ability the sturgeon possessed—the ability to adapt—showed the will to survive. The world is always changing, she correctly believed, and to survive, everything must change with it. She was tracking change right now—big change—as the Asian Carp were knocking on the door of Lake Michigan.

Emily felt most at home when working in the waters contiguous with the Mississippi. Although there are 27 different species of sturgeon and eight species in North America, only three—the Pallid, Shovelnose, and the Lake Sturgeon spend their entire lives in freshwater. Lake Sturgeon evolved originally in the Mississippi.

Standing in water that leads to that river, both Lisa and Emily wore chest-high olive-green waders and light brown fishing vests. Lisa had very straight natural blond hair cascading past her shoulders. She was 5'-8" tall with a slight build. Emily was much shorter—5'-3" with an athletic build. Her hair was dark brown, medium length, with beautiful waviness.

News reporters and photojournalists were more interested in covering the Asian Carp story when they heard that Emily and Lisa were in the area. They were both knowledgeable and, importantly, photogenic. Asian Carp were not known for their looks, so it presented an interesting dichotomy when Emily and Lisa were photographed holding these fish. A portion of their work involved taking water samples and testing those samples for DNA evidence showing that Asian Carp were in the vicinity. They had worked their way up river—

Lisa, Emily, and the carp. It was the biologists' job to document how far the carp had come and to theorize how far up the rivers they potentially could be. They used two methodologies: telemetry and EDNA testing.

By capturing and tagging carp, the carp could be followed. Sensors on the banks of a waterway sent signals to their lab. Monitoring the movement of the carp provided valuable information on their habits: how they moved, when they moved, and, most importantly, how much they moved. They always moved closer to Lake Michigan. This process of capturing, tagging, releasing, and monitoring the fish is called "telemetry." The carp, like criminals, wore electronic tethers, their whereabouts always known. But unlike reformed criminals, these fish did not know the perimeters to stay within. They were always on the run.

While telemetry provided absolute evidence that the fish had reached certain points, testing the waters for their DNA provided evidence they might be around. Lisa and Emily took water samples farther upriver than where the carp had been discovered. What they were looking for was EDNA. This is Environmental DNA. EDNA comes from body parts, feces, or vomit.

The sun was still high in the sky when Lisa asked Emily about wrapping things up on the river.

"I'm wondering if we have enough samples for today."

"Getting tired? We still have testing to do tonight."

"What do you think we'll find?" asked Lisa. "We did find evidence up the river from here, what…four miles… and that was a month ago."

"I think a gull yacked in the river. Ate an old carp."

"A gull? You mean a Larus canus?" asked Lisa.

"Oh man, I like it when you talk that way! Actually, I was thinking of a Larus hyperboreus."

"Ah, the Glaucous Gull—came down to visit?"

"Yeah, but maybe it was a Larus livens from California!" said Emily, winking at Lisa.

"The Yellow Footed? In Illinois? Right. Maybe not even a gull. Could be a Haliaeetus leucocephalus."

"A Bald Eagle. Sure enough," said Emily. "You win! Say, I'd like to get these waders off and just chill a bit. It's nice out. Let's just hang for a while."

"Okay. I get the chase lounge!"

They waded over to their portable station and helped each other off with the waders. Lisa got into the chase lounge and stretched out. She had a swim suit bottom on beneath her waders and a crop top covering the swim suit top. Emily walked behind the chase lounge and reached down to Lisa's top. "Sit up for a sec." Lisa leaned forward and Emily pulled off Lisa's crop top.

"There. Now you can work on your tan. Wow, we've been working hard today!"

"Yeah," responded Lisa. "They warned us about this in college."

CHAPTER TWO
THE CHICAGO BARRIERS

Emily and Lisa went back to the lab that evening and started testing their samples. The lab was in an old building in downtown Chicago, close to the Chicago River. The entire second floor of the building was rented by the Shedd Aquarium. Most of the floor was dedicated to research, but some of it was used for accounting for the aquarium.

"Either the testing equipment is off or else we have a lot of EDNA," said Emily.

"Indeed. We're never seen it like this. We better go back tomorrow and take more samples. We may have a problem," said Lisa.

"What's your hypothesis?" asked Emily.

"I think the carp must be that far up the river if there's this much EDNA," said Lisa.

"We've never seen so many samples positive—what—nine out of ten?" said Emily.

"But, if they have come this far up the river, we should be seeing some. This scat is floating downstream so maybe we should go upstream four miles to where we found the other positive samples. Let's look for the fish tomorrow, not their EDNA. Let's grab the boat and see what we can stir up."

"Okay—sounds like a good excuse to have some fun," said Emily. "Let's go for it!"

"Work," said Lisa. "Remember it's work."

"Work work work—that's all you ever think about," stated Emily. "And tomorrow we have to go boating."

"Let's go all the way up to the electric barriers," said Lisa.

"Let's go out and have a beer," recommended Emily. "We can talk fish there."

Lisa and Emily walked down to the Sidecorner Pub where the door to the pub was located off from an alley. The pub was not on an intersection corner; it was on the corner of a busy street and the alley. The pub had wooden tables three inches thick with past patrons' carvings embedded deeply into the wood, carvings so deep that one had to watch where a glass was set down. They scored the back booth next to the bathroom. Months ago, Emily had carved a fish in the center of the table. Lisa embellished it with cartoonish legs. This was their favorite booth because they could see patrons as they made their way to the john. Sitting together in the rear bench, facing the rest of the bar, they propped their feet up against the opposite bench.

Down the center of the narrow bar ran a row of tables with chairs. These were often used for large groups: the tables would be ganged together to make a large, long seating area. The rest of the seating was made up of booths with benches. Tiffany lamps hung from the ceiling—mismatched lamps made almost 100 years earlier. The lights were always dimmed. Dark wood on the walls created an intimate atmosphere. Oak plank flooring was distressed from the years of use, particularly from the winter use when snow was tracked in. On the ceiling, the original embossed tin was painted flat black. A few ceiling fans spun slowly and silently.

Two mugs of beer magically arrived at their table.

"I'm tired talking fish," said Emily. "Let's talk about anything else."

"What!? It's not just fish we're talking about, it's fish poop and guts and all of that. Besides," said Lisa, "we are on a mission to save America!"

"Well, America can wait until tomorrow. I'm ready to chill," said Emily.

The next day they got up early and towed a 21- foot AquaSport over to the launch at Lake Calumet, about 20 miles south of downtown Chicago. A donor had presented a new Ford F-150 Lariat 4 x 4 to the aquarium as a gift. It was equipped with a tow package which used the transmission to assist the brakes during stops. It was a great vehicle and towed the AquaSport effortlessly. Emily backed the boat into the water after Lisa made sure that the drainplug was installed tightly in the stern. Lisa secured the boat to the dock as Emily parked the truck and trailer.

Equipped with two 150 HP Mercruisers hanging from the transom board, in smooth water it would get up to plane in ten seconds. Planer boards on the rear could be used when cruising slowly to keep the bow down. A very capable boat, but utilitarian, it was able to navigate virtually any waterway, no matter how rough. It had a deep V bow. Waves might cascade over the bow, but drains in the stern would exhaust the water as quickly as it came in. The entire boat was made of thick fiberglass.

Similar in design to a Boston Whaler, there was a center console with the steering wheel, controls, and gauges. Usually the pilot and lookout stood behind this console, although there was a fiberglass seat. By standing, Lisa and Emily had a better view of the waters. Brackets supporting the windshield tied down into the sides of the console, serving as handholds to steady oneself as the boat leapt through challenging waters. Lisa and Emily stood with the back of their knees pressed against the seat, steadying their selves. This helped to control their bodies' forward/backward motion. They stood with their legs slightly spread, to help balance and to counteract side-to-side motion. With their knees slightly bent, their legs acted as shock absorbers.

Passengers could sit in a fiberglass unpadded seat in front of the console. Or, they could sit up in the bow of the boat on top of lids covering livewells, but sitting there usually meant getting wet because of the splashing inside.

Carefully, because of the shallow depth, Lisa navigated the AquaSport out of Lake Calumet and into the Calumet-Sag Channel. These were dredged areas where proper attention to the red and green buoys was important. "Remember: 'red buoy on the right' when going up river, but we're going down because they changed the course of the river a hundred years ago, so the red should be on the left," said Lisa. "Did they screw everything up or what?"

"We wouldn't have a job if they didn't screw it up," replied Emily. "The carp wouldn't be able to get to Lake Michigan and no one would care."

"Except for all those people downstream who are already affected," said Lisa.

"That's history now. We have to worry about not letting it get any worse. The future is in our hands," said Emily.

"Comforting. That is really comforting. The future is in our hands. A couple of post-grads with nothing better to do than to protect the Chicago waterways looking for fish crap."

"No one else is doing it," said Emily. "We need to do the best that we can."

"The electric fish barriers and you and me…we are the last resort. If the electric barriers don't do it, I don't know what's going to happen," said Lisa. "They should be doing more."

Emily and Lisa went down the channel to the Lower Chicago Sanitary and Ship Canal. This river had also been reversed a hundred years earlier. It used to flow into the Upper Chicago Sanitary and Ship Canal, then into Lake Michigan. By tying these rivers into the Mississippi, no one imagined a problem like this would occur. Before the connection, branches of the Mississippi petered out in Illinois and Minnesota. There was no connection between Lake Michigan and the Mississippi.

Lake Michigan is connected to the other Great Lakes—Lakes Superior, Huron, Ontario, and Erie. After pouring over Niagara Falls and through Lake Ontario, the water flows to the Atlantic. The tail end of the Mississippi drains into the Atlantic at the Gulf of Mexico. Now the beginning of the Mississippi—through the Great Lakes—led to the more northern region of the Atlantic. Eventually the carp could work their way over there—if they could survive the plunge over Niagara Falls.

Turning left from the Lower Chicago Sanitary and Ship Canal, they went past the water treatment plant at Lemont and over to the Barrier One Electric Fish Barrier. The U.S. Army Corps of Engineers electrified the water near Chicago to attempt to stop the migration of the carp into Lake Michigan.

This was the barrier of last resort—if the fish got past this one, they had clear access to Lake Michigan.

"Let's see if we can feel the pulse of the grid," said Emily.

They passed over the grid, a mesh design that is constructed and then lowered down into the canal where it rests on the bottom. On the banks are stations controlling the electricity.

"Currently," said Lisa, "no pun intended, it operates at 1 volt/inch, 5 hertz, which is cycles per second, and 4 ms, which stands for pulse duration in milliseconds. They keep changing it to test what works best."

"So," said Emily, "I hope they have the hertz and milliseconds right!"

"That is the plan. Do not forget about the one volt per inch—that might be important, too," said Lisa.

They cruised past the electric barriers without feeling any effects, continuing toward the area they had tested yesterday. That was 30 miles downstream. If they found what they were looking for, they would find an Asian Carp before they reached yesterday's testing area.

"I'll make you a bet," said Emily, "that we find an Asian Carp a few miles upstream from where we were yesterday."

"Which species?"

"Silver—'cause they are easy to spot," said Emily.

"Those are the worst ones—flying carp."

"Yeah, like 'Holy Flying Carp, Batman!'" said Emily.

"So there's the Silver, Bighead, Grass, and the Black Carp—which do you dislike the most?"

"Well, let's see. The Silver jumps out of the water as much as eight feet, so that's pretty impressive. The Bighead is the largest, has the most eggs and is the most voracious. The Grass and the Black are sort of just along for the ride, so, I'd say maybe the Bighead because it has so many eggs," said Emily.

"I'm going with the Silver because it jumps. That's frightening!"

"Do you think they could ever cross-breed? Make a hybrid?" asked Emily.

"A heterozygous carp? They would have allelomorph genes—alternate forms."

"Like a burro. Or, remember seeing the picture of the liger—half lion/half tiger?"

"Yes, and ligers are not sterile, like many hybrids. And, they weigh more than any other cat—up to 900 pounds!"

"Maybe get a huge Bighead/Silver Carp that would breed like mad and would jump out of the water? Sort of like a sailfish flying through the air. A megacarp!"

"Ahhhhhh! A megacarp! It could eat small children."

"I'm glad they're filter-feeders."

"How about the Grass and the Black, though. They might be able to chew you to death!"

"Chomp, chomp, chomp."

Attached to the AquaSport was a netting system with two long poles that could be swung out from the side of the boat. It was controlled by an arrangement of ropes and pulleys to raise or lower the nets. Lisa shifted into neutral. "Let's see what we can scoop up."

They lowered the nets into the water and started drifting downstream. Every few minutes they would raise the nets to see what they caught. "A lot of bass in this river," said Emily.

Indeed, looking over the edge of the boat, schools of bass were abundant. They checked their nets and released their catch back into the river. They were upstream ten miles from where they were yesterday, then they netted their first Asian Carp—it was a Grass Carp.

"Well, then," said Emily, "that proves it—if there's a Grass Carp, probably there's a Silver, Black, and Bighead somewhere around here. And we're just twenty miles down from the fish barrier."

"Is it tagged?" asked Emily.

"No tag, so who knows where it came from."

"Ugly guy, huh?"

"Not too pretty."

Emily notated the location of their find. "They are getting closer and closer to Chicago—it's only a matter of time until they are up to the grid."

Lisa tagged the carp and sent it on its way.

"Remember: tomorrow we have that lecture to do," said Emily.

CHAPTER THREE
THE LECTURE

The Shedd Aquarium often hosted lectures to inform the public about Asian Carp. Lisa and Emily normally would handle these lectures. They were good speakers and could modify the presentations based on the demographics of their audience. The audience could consist of school children interested in fish or scientists wanting to learn the latest developments. Today, college students from the University of Chicago made up the audience.

Emily usually started the lectures, warming up the audience. Lisa handled the nitty-gritty. They both wore light brown field outfits and high brown leather boots with the pants tucked into the boots, making them look like seasoned, hands-on explorers. They found that this increased their credibility.

Emily: So good to have all of you here. We really love giving these presentations because most of the time we're out wading through the rivers looking for carp poop. Don't get us wrong. We love looking for carp poop, but every now and then it's good to share our findings with others. By that, I don't mean we are going to share the poop with you. No! We are just going to tell you about it and why it is important to us.

Lisa: Thanks for that, Emily. Now there's a gal that takes poop seriously. Well, so do I and that's why we get along so well. What we're doing, first of all, is looking for the signs the carp have reached certain areas. If we find their poop, it can mean they are in the vicinity.

Emily: Birds that eat carp will partially digest the carp's DNA, then may excrete it into the river. This is why when we find DNA it means the carp are probably around but not necessarily. What we are looking for is called Environmental DNA. This can be carp poop or portions of the actual carp that may have been eaten and then ended up in the river. You get the idea. Usually we break for lunch at this point.

Lisa: Some carp are indigenous to this area. We are not interested in those carp. They are doing no harm. We are looking for Asian Carp. There are four types of Asian Carp that are invasive species. Emily.

Emily: Don't look at me. I'm not one of them.

Lisa: I meant, why don't you tell us about the four species.

Emily: Oh. Well, there's the Silver Carp. This is the one you may have seen pictures of. It jumps as much as eight feet out of the water. They can grow to be five feet long. Then, there's the Bigheaded Carp. This one can lay over a million eggs during its lifetime. Both of these carp feed on phytoplankton and zooplankton. Does anybody know what zooplankton is? Young lady over there, she said, pointing.

Audience member: Zooplankton is a group that includes bacteria—the smallest member of the group—and also includes krill that Baleen whales feed on, and the group includes jellyfish that can grow as large as six feet in diameter.

Lisa: Wow. Do you need a job! You're right. And, jellyfish was my specialty in college. Now, just so you know, these species also eat phytoplankton, which is plant matter, like algae. You can remember it like this: zooplankton is the category made up of animal forms—think of the animals in the zoo. Phytoplankton is the category made up of plant forms. "Phyto" comes from the Greek word meaning "wanderer." They just drift with the currents. The Silver Carp and the Bigheaded are filter feeders, just as are the Baleen whales you mentioned. They swim through the water, filtering out zooplankton and phytoplankton. There's two other species we are looking for—the Grass Carp, which eats grassy stuff and the Black Carp, which eats small clams, mussels, and stuff like that. Those two species have special teeth in the back of their mouth to crush up their food. These are called pharyngeal teeth.

Emily: These carp were imported from Asia for a specific purpose. In 1984, a catfish farmer in Arkansas had an algae problem with his ponds. Since the carp eat algae, he brought these fish in to control the algae. One week, large rains came and the ponds overflowed into the Mississippi River. These carp have traveled up the river 1,500 miles to Chicago. It's our job to try to stop them from getting into Lake Michigan.

Lisa: They eat so much—about 40% of their body weight every day—they out-compete our native fish for food, so, eventually, all we might have left in Lake Michigan are carp! When local species are made extinct, it is called extirpation.

Emily: Since the Silver Carp jump into the air, sports such as water skiing would not be recommended. Who would want to be water skiing and smacked in the face with an 80-pound carp—please raise your hands! Say Lisa, would you like to show off and rattle off the scientific names of the four species of carp?

Lisa: Sure.

Emily: Silver?

Lisa: Hypopthalmichthys molitrix.

Emily: Bigheaded?

Lisa: Hypopthalmichthys nobilis.

Emily: Black?

Lisa: Mylopharyngodon piceus.

Emily: Grass?

Lisa: Ctenopharyngodon idella. Notice that the Black and Grass, with the pharyngeal teeth, have a portion of the word pharyngeal in their Latin names. By seeing things like this, it's easier to remember the names.

Emily: The word pharyngeal comes from the part of the body where the throat, nasal passages, and esophagus all come together. That's our pharynx.

Emily: We sometimes play games quizzing each other on Latin names so that we remember them.

Lisa: That sounds a little nerdy.

Emily: I just like to hear her say those big words! Now Lisa, should we eat a carp for lunch?

Lisa: Carp are not good to eat. And, they are difficult to clean. They have an extra set of bones, as pike do, that makes it impossible to filet them. These are the intramuscular bones. Questions?

Audience member: What's being done to stop them from getting into Lake Michigan?

Lisa: Electric grids have been installed in Romeoville, just south of Chicago. These grids send off electric impulses that deter the fish from getting up the river and into Lake Michigan. We monitor these areas to make sure that the fish have not breached the electric grids. We were over checking things out around the grids yesterday.

Emily: There are three grids so that if one grid needs to be shut down, there are still two in operation.

Audience member: How far up the river have the carp come?

Lisa: We are finding that they have almost reached the grids. We have not found them beyond the grids. We found a Grass Carp twenty miles from the grid yesterday.

Emily: The Chicago River was connected into the Mississippi over a hundred years ago. Chicago connected it to get rid of their sewage. Is it time for lunch now, Lisa?

Audience member: How was it connected?

Lisa: The eastern valley of America's continental divide runs right through Chicago—it sort of peters out here. With a bit of explosives and excavation, the river was made to run backwards and into the Mississippi. Chicago has always taken their drinking water from Lake Michigan. This way, they weren't dumping their waste into the same area they were sucking their drinking water from. Lunchtime, yet?

Emily: There were two environmental mistakes: 1) The connection of the Mississippi into Lake Michigan. 2) The introduction of Asian Carp to America. Nobody knew at the time—it never could have been imagined. But, these two mistakes are now multiplying into a possible ecological disaster.

Lisa: What this tells us is this: Before we alter our environment, we need to think through the ramifications of our actions. Long range. Imagine what seems impossible. By imagining the impossible, we may discover what is possible.

Emily: Thanks for coming to this discussion. Come back again. We have new information to share all the time. Every day, it seems, Lisa and I discover new things.

Lisa: Emily and I are signing photographs in the gift shop. We have a great shot with both of us holding up an 80# Silver Carp. All proceeds go to the Shedd, even though we thought we should get a cut of the action.

CHAPTER FOUR
THE BIG RAIN

Throughout the next season, Emily and Lisa monitored the advances of the carp. At this point, it wasn't a matter of if the carp would reach the electric grids in Romeoville—it was simply a matter of when. Their testing showed that all four species were gradually making their way up the river. By the end of the season, they were all up to the grid. There wasn't just one, or two, or three, or four. Hundreds at first, then thousands were being held back by the grid. The optimists held the opinion that this proved the effectiveness of the system, while the pessimists wondered how the grid would permanently hold back so many fish. It was like a log jam.

With the AquaSport patrolling the waters, the props of the Mercury 150 outboards ground up so many carp, it was as though they had been put through blenders. "Carp soup," is what they named it. Live carp swam through the carp soup without fear that they may be the next ingredient. Lisa and Emily watched as carp picked away at the pieces of their former pals. "I think they are developing a taste for each other," Emily said. "Why should they look for their normal food when there's so much floating around in the waters?"

"Lots of fish cannibalize each other," said Lisa. "In fact, some species cannibalize almost of their own young."

"No respect," said Emily. "I'm glad my parents didn't eat me."

"Probably when you were in junior high they wondered why they hadn't," said Lisa.

"I was worse in high school, actually," said Emily. "I was a late bloomer."

"I was consistent. I gave my parents hell throughout junior high and high school. They threatened me with military school once. Even got brochures for a couple and left them out where I would find them."

"You were just a free spirit, that's all," said Emily. "You turned out great. You still are a free spirit. There's nothing wrong with that."

"Everybody works through it. Most people, anyways. It's just a challenge going through school. You're changing so much it's hard to keep up with yourself. That's all."

"Like running downhill too fast?"

"Yeah, it's like that."

"Everything's always changing," said Emily. "Look at all the carp here."

Their new assignment was to monitor the river upstream of the grids to make sure that no carp had breached the system. Open water to Lake Michigan was at the head of the river. They set up receivers on the banks to receive signals if any tagged carp breached the system. All three grids were working perfectly. No signals were ever received.

"As long as things keep working like this, things may be okay," said Lisa, "but there is that wall of carp at the grid."

"It's like the invisible fencing for dogs. You know—the buried wire in the ground. The dog has a shock collar on it. Most dogs won't breach the system," said Emily.

"But some do," stated Lisa. "I've heard of dogs chasing a deer and taking the hit."

"Yeah, they do it without thinking about it. I wonder what these fish are thinking. Do you think they think?" asked Emily.

"Maybe. When we come through with the AquaSport they probably say, 'Hey, watch out Sam, you saw what happened to Harold, didn't you? He got chopped up with the prop last week!'"

"Yeah, I remember," he'd say. "Sure did taste good!"

Lisa laughed. "Those fish have to wonder what's on the other side."

On a Tuesday that spring, it began to rain. A large storm system blanketed the entire Midwest. Two inches of rain fell on the first day; three inches on the next day. All of the rivers started to reach flood stage. On Thursday, another three inches of rain fell. In the Chicago area, the typical annual rainfall is thirty-three inches. With eight inches in three days, many rivers began to crest their banks. The storm sewer systems began to back up—introducing water into the streets instead of taking it away. Many of the streets in the downtown portions of Chicago began to flood.

Emily and Lisa started driving toward the affected areas. They both brought knee-high rubber boots.

"Remember what happened in Grand Rapids," said Lisa. "2013. The Grand River breached its banks and flooded out everything by the river. One guy looked out his condo window and it was like he was looking into an aquarium. The water was three feet up on the window. A fish was swimming by."

"Yeah. Michigan. The Grand River runs right through Grand Rapids. They thought that the bridges might get washed away—the water was pressing up against the arches of the bridges."

"They parked a train on the railroad bridge to weigh it down. That was risky though. I read that if the plan hadn't worked and the bridge would have failed, the train cars would have ended up like a huge dam in the river and would have backed it up worse—then the other bridges might have failed," said Lisa.

"All hell would have broken loose!" said Emily.

"All hell did break loose—when you're seeing fish swim by your condo window!" said Lisa.

"Well, let's see how the streets of Chicago are faring. Good thing the Sidecorner Pub is on high ground—at least that place will be okay!"

"A few blocks east of there—that's where the street takes that dip. That's where I'm thinking we should go," said Lisa.

"I know the street must be flooded. Let's take our nets and see if there's anything swimming around."

They drove past the area with the dip and could see it was flooded. After parking the truck, Lisa and Emily grabbed their nets, pulled on knee-high boots and started walking toward the area. Cars had tried to make it through the roadway but had stalled and now were blocking the road. People had rafts and flat-bottomed boats, salvaging belongings out of their storefronts and homes. With almost two feet of water in the street, the biologists' boots were just high enough. "Sort of looks like the apocalypse," said Lisa.

"The end of the world as we knew it."

"This is how it'll look after the polar caps melt!"

"It'll look worse!"

"Looks like France with the Seine River running through it."

"Need a gondola with some cute guy standing up paddling and singing."

"Need to get that car out of the way."

"See any fish?"

"No. Want to drag the nets around?"

"Sure. I don't see anything."

"Some trash."

"Washed up from the storm sewer system. Look—the water is coming up through the curb grate instead of going down into it."

"Sort of like a geyser."

"Where was that—the sewer lids, you know—the manhole covers—they popped up from the water pressure and sort of floated down the street a few feet?"

"I heard of that. Cast iron floating!"

"So, what if that happened here?"

"You're scaring me. We could be walking around and drop inside a manhole!"

"Would you save me?" asked Emily.

"Oh sure. Dive in right after you," said Lisa.

"What a way to go!"

"Let's walk on the curb. There's never any manholes on the curb," said Lisa.

"It's higher, too. My boots are just high enough. Let's bring our waders tomorrow."

"Good idea."

"I don't see any fish. Just a bunch of muddy water."

"What a mess!"

"Hey look!"

There was a young boy, about ten years old, sitting by his second story window. He had a fishing pole with a line and bobber, the bobber floating in the water.

"Any luck?" yelled Emily. The boy shook his head no, smiled, and waved.

"You know," said Lisa, "I bet he never thought he'd be fishing in the comfort of his living room!"

Getting back in the truck, they drove around notating which streets had flooded and approximately how deep the water was in each street. Tomorrow they would come back and see what, if anything, had changed.

The next morning they got up before dawn and drove down to the worst-hit areas. With their waders on and each with a net, they got out of the truck and started walking toward the low areas. They turned the corner where the street started going downhill and, in the dark, they could hear splashing.

"What's that?" asked Lisa.

"Splashing. It's not fish jumping, is it?"

The sky was just beginning to lighten. It was difficult to gauge the situation. They approached the splashing sound and could see, by the streetlights, that the street was populated by fish.

"Silver Carp. Look at them," said Lisa.

"They are everywhere!"

Silver Carp, some three foot long, were jumping out of the water. In those areas where the water tapered off as the street elevated, carp were half in the water and half out of the water, using their pectoral fins to push their selves along. They squirmed, too, using their tail to propel themselves.

"I don't even want to get my waders wet," said Emily.

"Might get knocked down by a fish."

"In the middle of the street!"

"Who would have thought?"

"Well, we thought about it yesterday. Give us some credit!"

"But I never thought it would be like this. Not in my wildest dreams," said Lisa.

"Your wildest dreams are about carp?"

"Nope," said Lisa. "Not even close."

CHAPTER FIVE
THE FISH KILL

"You know," said Emily, "we should let it get light out. This is scary. Let's go out and get breakfast and come back. I'm freaking out."

Up a few blocks, on higher ground, was a 24-hour restaurant known for their breakfasts. Lisa and Emily walked to the restaurant with their waders still on, nets balanced on their shoulders. They took off their waders and left them, with their nets, by the door to the restaurant. "Who would ever think that we'd be here with waders on?" said Emily. "Ridiculous!"

After breakfast, they walked back to their truck and drove around, checking on the areas they had seen flooded the day before. In many of the streets they could see fish jumping even without getting out of the truck. Lisa called the Corps of Engineers to let them know what was happening.

"Look," said Lisa. "We are going to meet with engineering this morning to look at how this storm sewer system is laid out, but our worry is that some of the storm sewers dump into the canal after the electric grid. This is the problem: how are the fish going to be contained by the grid if the fish aren't even in the river? Think about a fish kill and it'd have to be done quick!"

After meeting with engineering, they were convinced. The storm sewer systems were interconnected. Although they were designed to all lead away from Lake Michigan, with the sewers full of water (and fish) the fish had a route where they could bypass the grid. The Corps of Engineers jumped into action.

Preparing to poison the river, they concocted a deadly mixture of Rotenone—2,500 gallons worth—and starting at the mouth of the river right at Lake Michigan, began to spread the poison. By starting at the mouth of the river, fish attempting to escape the poison would be chased back away from Lake Michigan. Rotenone works as a piscicide by preventing the gills of fish from absorbing oxygen. The poison would kill every living thing in the river—every fish, snail, clam, crayfish—everything, but it was the right thing to do.

It stopped raining the next day and the water in the streets began to recede. Cars, trucks, and busses could now navigate through all of the streets even though there were a few inches of water, and lots of fish, left in the streets. Although thousands of fish had made it up into the streets through the storm sewer, not all of them made it back down. They ended up in the middle of the street or over by the curb. The cars, trucks, and busses, as they traveled down the streets, ran over the fish. Some people tried to drive around them, but there were too many, so most people simply drove over them, spreading fish guts up and down the downtown streets of Chicago.

In the river, the Rotenone had taken its toll. It was estimated that there were 250,000 fish floating in the canal. On the bottom, hundreds of thousands of snails, clams, and crayfish were dead. The surface of the river showed the results—no water could be seen—it was solid dead fish.

The clouds went away and the sun started shining brightly. Temperatures soared. The streets dried up, leaving only the smashed up remains of the fish. Fish guts were everywhere. With the higher temperatures, the smell was unimaginable. The fish in the river began to bloat and explode. So did the fish that hadn't been run over on the streets. The mayor called a city emergency. Crews came out with backhoes, dump trucks, sweepers, and street cleaners. The fire department hooked up their hoses to the hydrants and flushed the remainder down the drains. It took three days to rid the streets of the dead fish.

Lisa and Emily insisted that even more Rotenone was needed in the river.

"What if," they said, "some of the fish eggs that are being washed down the storm sewer are already fertilized? They are being washed into the river. Couldn't the fertilized eggs get into Lake Michigan?"

More Rotenone was placed in the river. "I still have a bad feeling about this," said Lisa. "Out of all of these fish, there has to be some that got through. And what if one was pregnant?"

The Corps installed a wall of grinders across the river, about two miles down from Lake Michigan. The grinders looked like huge wood-chippers. They had wide flared mouths twelve feet across. Hiring a fleet of tugboats, they bolted large steel perforated planks on the front of the boats. The tugboats had a job: push this wall of carp through the grinders. The boats lined up across the river, starting at the mouth of the river at Lake Michigan and began to move toward the grinders. Carp guts flew forty feet into the air as they were forced through the grinders. The water behind the grinders turned reddish-purple, the water thick as pea soup.

The tugboats made three passes, effectively getting all of the floating carp to rip through the grinders. The grinders were then removed and the tugboats started forcing the carp soup downriver, just to get it away from the city.

"Still," said Lisa. "I still have bad feelings about this."

CHAPTER SIX
TWO YEARS LATER

Inevitably, all four species of carp began to establish themselves in Lake Michigan. It could have been the fertilized eggs that made it through, or maybe a few carp made a run for it before the Rotenone was installed. There were tens of millions of carp in the Mississippi—everybody knew that—it was simple mathematics. If 250,000 had died by only poisoning just two miles of the river right before the entrance to Lake Michigan, how many were left in the other 2,530 miles of the Mississippi? The numbers alone seemed to make it obvious: the carp would somehow make it into Lake Michigan.

Emily had discussed this possibility with many people, but one conversation haunted her. The expert she was discussing this with stated with absolute conviction that there was a "one in a million" possibility that a carp could get into Lake Michigan. Emily had answered it this way: "If there is a one chance in a million, then we're doomed, because there are tens of millions of carp in the Mississippi and adjoining rivers. One single Bigheaded Carp produces one million eggs. There's the one in a million."

Maybe there were hundreds of millions of carp in the rivers. That was history. What was important now was

Lake Michigan. Emily's and Lisa's new assignment was to monitor how many carp had become established in Lake Michigan and how quickly they were spreading. They were getting a lot of use out of the AquaSport. They needed to tag as many carp as possible.

The old system of telemetry was outmoded. That had been developed to monitor fish in rivers, with the sensors set up on the banks. Lake Michigan is eighty miles across at its narrowest. The sensors on the banks of the rivers could only sense a fish 1,000 feet away. That wasn't going to work. Lisa came up with the idea first: work with the cell phone companies and their satellites. Have their satellites capture the signals sent from the tagged carp. This way, a carp in the middle of Lake Michigan would be identified. Reworking the sensors, Lisa developed a sensor that would capture a signal from water as deep as 200 feet. The cell phone companies were given financial incentives as well as the opportunity to portray themselves as do-gooders. They were, as one stated emphatically in a Super Bowl ad, "Helping America protect its valuable resources." Another company said that they were "aiding in the scientific research for the good of the world." It almost made you want to run up some extra minutes.

Emily saw some irony in their relationship with the cell phone companies. As they tagged and released the carp, the computer map of Lake Michigan started to show greater coverage—like the map of the United States the competing phone companies have to show how great their coverage is. In the case of Lake Michigan, though, less coverage was better. Less became more as the carp tightened their stronghold on the lake.

Lisa and Emily continued to tag and release carp.

"I'm hoping," said Emily, "that somehow the carp will not want to wander from Lake Michigan."

"What? Go into Lake Huron?" asked Lisa as she threw another tagged carp overboard.

"Yep, through the Straits of Mackinac."

"They could set up another grid there."

"Deep water and over five miles in width, isn't it?"

"Yeah. Might be a little tough. The bridge there connecting the Lower Peninsula to the Upper Peninsula of Michigan is the longest suspension bridge between anchorages in the western hemisphere."

"Longer than the Golden Gate?"

"Yep. Beautiful too."

"Hang the grid from the bridge—another engineering marvel!"

"Wait. Caught another carp. Look at this one. She's ready to pop!"

The biologists did not tag pregnant carp. If a fish was determined to be pregnant, its belly was sliced open and the eggs dumped into a five-gallon bucket. The fish was then heaved overboard. Chefs had tried to find ways to cook up these carp eggs, but fine caviar they were not. There were contests to create the best recipes, but the winning recipe always was determined to be less than great. The results of these contests were often donated to the homeless shelters in the area. Fewer people began arriving to the shelters, and a spike in employment resulted. Some days Lisa and Emily would fill up six or seven of these buckets. The buckets were taken to the landfill for disposal.

All of the states bordering Lake Michigan issued unlimited fishing permits for Asian Carp. Fisherman would catch as much as 1,000 pounds of carp in a day. Any type of fishing was allowed: you could hook them, snag them, spear them, net them, club them or get creative. Since the Silver Carp jumped out of the water, bow hunting developed into a new sport. Cross-bows, especially, proved to be a fun way to fish.

Recycling stations were built next to all of the boat launches. They were essentially large garbage disposals with a container feature. You'd dump in the day's catch and it would get ground up and packaged into thick 40# heat-sealed plastic bags with a handle. Most of it was used as fertilizer but some of it ended up as food for pigs—known to eat anything. One pet food distributor tried to market cat food with the slogan, "It's carpalicious," but it didn't fly. A vitamin company squeezed the oil from carp, concentrated it, and put it in a capsule. You were supposed to take one every day so they named it "Carpe Diem." This didn't go over either. No one could figure out a good use for the carp.

In Newbury, Michigan, during the winter festival, there developed a carp-throwing contest. The rules were simple: whoever threw the carp the farthest won a prize. There were several divisions. Starting with the youngest, those up to five years old could throw any carp up to five pounds. Those up to ten could throw ten-pound carp. Those from eleven to fifteen years old could throw a carp up to fifteen pounds. Those sixteen to twenty could throw a twenty-pound carp. Twenty-one and older had to throw a carp between twenty-one pounds and twenty-five pounds. After that was the heavy-weight division, open to all ages. A carp over forty pounds was attached to a six foot long rope and was slung for distance.

To insure fairness to all, there were men's divisions and lady's divisions, and the well-attended senior's divisions.

By the end of summer, Lisa and Emily started to notice a trend: the fish they were catching were growing very rapidly. When they caught a tagged fish, they were surprised by how much it had grown. Also, they started catching record-breaking sizes.

"This is my theory," said Lisa. "You know how if you buy a goldfish and keep him in a small bowl, the fish won't grow too much, as if he doesn't want to outgrow his environment. However, if you put that fish in a large aquarium, he grows quickly. These carp have never been in a body of water as large as Lake Michigan—it is the largest body of fresh water on earth—I'm thinking that they are taking advantage of its size."

"Largest? Lake Superior is over 31,000 square miles!"

"Technically Lake Michigan and Lake Huron are the same lake, connected at the straits—that makes it larger than Lake Superior. Something like 45,000 square miles."

"Well how big could these fish get?" asked Emily.

"I'm thinking that it may only be limited by their food supply. If the Silvers and Bigheaded start to run out of phytoplankton and zooplankton, their growth rate should slow down."

"Man, we should have been measuring that all along, then," said Emily.

"We've been so busy, we didn't think of it. Until now."

"The Blacks and the Grass may also be depleting their food supplies a bit, so their growth rates may slow down, too. I suppose we should start checking that stuff, too, huh? Boy," said Emily, "I sure do long for the lazy days along the river looking for EDNA."

"Yeah," said Lisa. "Those were the days."

CHAPTER SEVEN
THE METAMORPHOSIS

During the next two summers, there were several developments. Their theory about the carp's food source diminishing was correct. The carp were eating themselves out of food. The ramifications of this were that the carps' growth rates stabilized. Now, Lisa and Emily started to notice different changes in how the carp looked. The dorsal fin on the top of their bodies was beginning to grow. Their pectoral fins, toward the front of their bodies and down low, were also starting to grow. Their mouths were starting to take on a different shape.

They noticed that the pharyngeal teeth were starting to develop extra branches. They usually had what was called a "2-4-2" pattern, where the tooth structure had a set of two teeth, then a set of four, then another set of two. Now, there were branches off from each set.

The pharyngeal teeth, always back by the throat of the Black and Grass Carps, had begun to move forward in their mouths. In the Silver and Bighead Carp, which never had any teeth, small teeth were starting to erupt in the front of their mouths. In all four species, their mouths were adjusting upward. Their eyes, too, were moving higher on their bodies.

It appeared that the original distinguishing characteristics of each specie were becoming less apparent. The species were merging, taking on the preferred attributes of each specie, just as different breeds of canines when bred together generally assume the more positive characteristics of each breed. In this case, though, what could be a positive characteristic when you're a fish may differ from when you're a biologist looking at the evolution. From the fish's point of view, they were adapting to their new environment: one in which there was less phytoplankton and zooplankton and fewer grasses and fewer mussels. The fish were exhausting their own food supply.

The digestive system was changing, too. The carp had no stomach—just a long intestine—which accounted for the massive quantities of food consumed. Everything went right through them. Now, though, an actual stomach was developing. In the fall, Lisa dissected a carp and found a small fish inside its gut.

"They're evolving," said Lisa.

"They didn't have enough to eat and now they've changed diets," said Emily.

"They needed a food source."

"So now they're going to start eating each other. I wonder how that's going to turn out."

"Only time will tell. Only time will tell."

Big changes came the next summer. Mainly, the carp no longer searched the waters for their original food source—they started eating fish. The carp ate perch, bass, pike, salmon, and each other. Since they always ate so much, now that they had a reliable food source, their growth rate was amazing. Lisa and Emily began catching record sizes—sixteen feet long and 300 pounds. Fish were eating fish almost half their size. Two-foot long fish were eating one-foot long fish. Four-foot long fish were eating two-foot long fish. The carp seemed to prefer eating the game fish in Lake Michigan. Whereas anglers used to flock to Lake Michigan for perch and in the fall for Coho Salmon, these fish didn't exist anymore. For Lake Michigan, these fish were extirpated.

The species continued to blend characteristics. Although the Silver Carp were originally the only ones to jump out of the water, now the others were starting to breach the surface. The Silver Carp started producing as many eggs as the Bigheaded. And they all continued to develop more teeth.

Lisa and Emily noticed that they were also becoming more aggressive. Before when they were brought into the boat, they would flop around and try to jump a bit; now they were actually snapping at them. After Lisa got bit badly one day, they started wearing armored gloves whenever they handled the fish.

Also, their fins continued to grow.

CHAPTER EIGHT
GOING TO GRAND HAVEN

The following summer, Lisa and Emily were transferred over to the eastern shore of Lake Michigan, the Michigan side. The water is warmer over there. The wind usually blows from the west, blowing the warmer water off from the surface over to the sandy shores on the Michigan side.

The beach towns there thrive during the summer—at least they used to when fishing was good. Still, the boating industry was doing okay and those beautiful sandy beaches were packed with sunbathers. There was some surfing, too. Along the piers jutting out into the water, the waves grew and surfers could catch some pretty good waves. They are a hearty group, sometimes surfing late into the fall when the waves are the largest. Decked out in wet suits, the air and the water could be 40 degrees and still the pier area was packed with surfers.

The piers jutted out into Lake Michigan in those areas where rivers dumped into the lake. The rivers were continually dredged to allow for large ships to deliver their goods. In Grand Haven, for example, the Grand River terminates after running through most of Michigan. This is the river that flooded Michigan's second largest city, Grand Rapids, in 2013. Freighters come from across the lake delivering coal and limestone, taking a load of sand back to Milwaukee for use in the foundries. There is a port a mile up the river where the off-loading and loading is accomplished.

Emily and Lisa would be stationed in Grand Haven, a five-block town that fronts on the Grand River and contains a state park on Lake Michigan. The ranger station at the edge of the park used to be for the rangers, but with the parks getting their budgets cut, the station had been rented out to visitors. This year, though, it was offered to Lisa and Emily for their home base. It was a 1,200 square-foot ranch right on Harbor Drive, close to the parking lot used by fishermen.

They towed the AquaSport through Chicago and up US 31, stopping by St. Joseph, South Haven, Saugatuck, and Holland on the way through. Grand Haven is across the lake from Milwaukee and just a bit south. Pulling in to the ranger station, they backed into the driveway and decided to tour the town.

Grand Haven was founded in 1834, early for a town in Michigan, but with the Grand River, Lake Michigan, and an abundance of timber, it was a boom town in its day. Fur trading was also a large industry. Indians inhabited the region and were willing to trade. There were government proclamations that declared that alcohol could not be part of any trade with Indians. It was put simply: "No liquor, or no trade." The Indians changed the proclamation to "No liquor, no trade." It was that simple. The pelts of beaver, fox, wolf, bear, muskrat, and other less-regarded animals such as raccoon and squirrel were all traded for the liquor and for items that they had a need for, mainly knives and firearms. These things would help them get more pelts to trade for more liquor, knives, and firearms.

The combination of liquor, knives, and firearms is not a good one. Eventually, of course, the Indians could not keep up with the advances of the white man. The industry turned to lumber, fueled by the need for lumber after the Chicago fire. Grand Haven helped to rebuild the second largest city in America.

Today, Grand Haven is about tourism. Before Memorial Day, not too much goes on, about as much as after Labor Day. June is not particularly a good month, so that really leaves July and August. Eight weeks to make it or break it. Grand Haven needs to take advantage of each of them.

Local businesses make the most of it while they can, are fair, don't rip anybody off, try to give everybody what they want, maybe charge too much for an ice cream cone now and again, but you don't sell much ice cream in the winter. In the winter, everything's discounted and the local bar may sell drinks for two bucks.

Emily and Lisa walked down the boardwalk from the ranger station. The boardwalk was parallel to Harbor Drive, running beside the Grand River. It connects the state park to downtown. Grand Haven developed the boardwalk thirty years ago. Before that, there was no real connection between the town on the Grand River and the state park on Lake Michigan.

The boardwalk leads to downtown, then past there to an area called Chinook Pier, which celebrates the salmon that were brought in. Especially in the fall when the salmon were running, the fishing industry was booming. That had all changed. With the carp, there were no salmon now, and Chinook Pier was a destination only for overpriced ice cream cones.

Emily and Lisa did not walk to Chinook Pier; they walked up a walkway with a forty-foot long brass map of the Grand River embedded in the exposed aggregate concrete. The map showed all of the tributaries running into the river and the towns built alongside it. Crossing the street, they came to the Kirby Grill.

"Great," said Emily. "The first place we come to is a bar. Let's go in."

"Well, don't you want to walk around downtown a bit first?"

"Later."

They went in the Kirby and ordered two whiskeys. Then two more.

After that, they decided to wait on the downtown tour. Better to do it straight.

Walking back on the boardwalk, they met some people they thought they may want to party with later. There were three couples, all from the area, college age, going to various colleges in the area. There is Western Michigan University in Kalamazoo, Calvin College in Grand Rapids, Hope College in Holland, and Grand Valley in Allendale. None of the couples went to the same college, so they seemed ready to have a bit of fun. For them, it was a long-distance relationship.

They invited the three couples back to their ranger station and learned quite a bit about each of them.

The first couple was Paul and Gina. Paul played football in high school and was disappointed that he could not make any college team. He was studying, if you could call it that, Physical Training. Mainly he just wanted to make it through college and maybe be a gym teacher. He was constantly working out. His girlfriend, Gina, was taking general studies and had no idea what she even wanted to major in. Maybe, she thought, she could teach kindergarten. Her friends teased her by saying then, at least, she would be smarter than most of her students. Gina was constantly touching up her nails and playing with her hair.

Joe and Betty were a lot smarter. Joe was a computer student and was very good at programming. He was a good-looking guy who kept himself in shape and would challenge Paul to wrestling matches. Betty was studying English and had a body that fluctuated in weight–she always looked good but she was constantly going on a new diet. She was afraid of becoming fat.

Ramsey and Cassandra had met in high school and continued their relationship in college. Ramsey wanted to become a cop. He was a large guy and was fearless. Cassandra played volleyball in college and was one of the team's best players, being tall and very athletic.

They all liked to smoke dope and drink, but Ramsey liked to keep the pot smoking on the down low.

Lisa and Emily explained to them why they were in town.

"What we are finding," explained Emily, "is that the carp are beginning to mutate. Whereas originally they were filter feeders, they now are fish of prey. They are developing teeth, are getting much larger, and their fins are getting proportionately larger. They are also becoming more aggressive."

Joe questioned the possibility of this occurring. "It takes thousands of years, millions sometimes for mutations to occur. It's impossible!"

"No," interrupted Lisa. "Species evolve and mutate quicker than anyone ever imagined. We just didn't realize it until recently. There was a recent study regarding swallows nesting by a busy highway. Within just a few years, the birds began developing shorter wings. The birds hit by cars were the ones with the longer wings. Theory was that the birds with shorter wings could dodge the cars better and passed this trait along as a means of survival."

"But that took generations," stated Cassandra.

"True," said Lisa. "But these fish seem to adapt quicker. It's more of a metamorphosis."

"There's a rule of science that's interesting," said Emily. "Once a species finds a viable niche, it tends to stay there—as long as the niche is available. There is no need for it to evolve. What we've found is that the carp have depleted...well...reduced their food supply so much that they needed to evolve quickly or they wouldn't survive."

"I saw this special on TV," said Gina as she played with her hair, "that some fish have eyes that move around all over their bodies!"

"Those are flounder, dear," said Paul gently. "And their eyes don't move all over their bodies, really. They just move from the sides of their head to the top of their head."

"That's right," said Lisa. "And it happens fast–within ten days."

"Like a butterfly," said Betty. "They turn from a caterpillar to a butterfly in ten days."

"Are they taking on the traits of the fish they eat? You are what you eat!" said Cassandra.

"Yeah maybe," said Emily. "We haven't thought about that. Anything seems possible. I'll tell ya, though, we have to be careful because the fish are getting aggressive. We're afraid of what might happen."

"Like what?" asked Gina.

"We don't even know. We don't know what's going to happen. We just keep taking samples and see that they are evolving," said Lisa.

"We find different things every day," said Emily. "We never know what we are going to discover! That's a cool part of this job."

"We're going to take the boat out tomorrow and see what we can find," said Ramsey.

"What kind do you have?" asked Lisa.

"Cigarette hull," said Ramsey. "42 foot. Twin 454's. Goes about ninety. It's my dad's, really. I ain't rich! Can hardly afford the fuel."

"Yeah baby!" said Cassandra. "It's too much fun."

"Well, be careful out there," warned Lisa.

The group stopped talking about fish and partied until 2:30 AM.

CHAPTER NINE
THE GRAND RIVER

Lisa and Emily slept in the next day. They were worn out by the previous 24 hours of activity. They went down to the Dee-lite Restaurant and split an order of Farmer's Hash. It was a fried up blend of eggs, potatoes, green peppers, and mushrooms with melted cheese on top. They drank several cups of coffee and felt like new.

They decided to take some time off and look around the town. Walking up Washington Street, which was the main downtown street, they visited several stores and became acquainted with the downtown area. After four blocks, there were no more stores—just the county building and Grand Haven City Hall. There were offices and businesses, banks and the post office, but the tony boutiques and small shops were all in the first four blocks.

This downtown area had recently undergone a transformation. It took almost two years to do, but the city completely tore up the first four blocks of road, sidewalk, curb and gutter and installed new infrastructure and pavement. They used exposed aggregate concrete for the walks and installed concrete planters and new streetlights. The downtown looked beautiful! Later they learned that the street and sidewalks were heated so there was no snow accumulation in the winter. The heat source for the water came from the power plant right across the river. The plant was required to cool the water it used in the process to make electricity before the water was released into the Grand River. By pumping it through pipes embedded in the streets and sidewalks, the cooling of the water provided a purpose.

They ended their tour of downtown by going into the Piano Factory—an old brick building that had been converted into shops and offices. Story and Clark pianos had been made there—high-end pianos lacquered black and polished smooth as glass. The brick on the inside of the building was sandblasted clean and left exposed. Huge beams supported the second floor above, over-structured for most everything, but structured correctly for a piano factory. The wooden floor was scarified from years of use—particularly from pianos being rolled down the wide hallways. On the walls were photographs showing how the building looked inside when it was used as a piano factory. Before it closed in 1984, sawdust and musical notes blew out the open windows and into the downtown street below. A blind man tuned the pianos for as long as anybody could remember, tuning them with a cadence that people couldn't help but step to as they walked through the downtown area. The sweet smell of glue—the real casein glue made from milk—surrounded the building.

Later that day, they hooked up the AquaSport and headed up the Grand River. The river was shallower than they had imagined. It had been dredged only eight miles upstream from where it dumped into Lake Michigan and they had to be aware of the marking buoys, staying between the red and green markers. They netted a few small carp and tossed them in the live well to keep them fresh—they would look them over after they returned to the ranger station. They decided to get a map of the Grand River because it was difficult to navigate. Much larger boats than the AquaSport were on the Grand River for that first eight miles, but the boats smaller than the AquaSport were actually better. They noticed that many of the boats were shallow vee or even flat-bottomed boats powered by short-shaft outboard motors. These boats could venture away from the dredged areas. They decided that they might rent such a boat next time they wanted to go up the river. The current was so slow they also considered kayaking.

"What would you think about not starting at Grand Haven?" asked Lisa. "Maybe we could rent kayaks and put them in the Grand River up by Grand Rapids and kayak down sometime."

"That's fifty miles!" said Emily. "I'm not kayaking fifty miles!"

"Hey, who said we would have to do it all in one day?"

"What? Take three days or something? Maybe there are some towns along the way with a motel or two. We could plan things out and just float downstream, taking some samples here and there. Where would we store the samples, though?"

"Maybe the motel would keep them on ice for us. Let's check things out and maybe spot a cooler here and there at the places we'll stay—talk to the owners, etc. Get a plan together. Then we'd have to go back upriver and pick up the samples with the truck. This might just work out."

"Don't say work. Let's make this fun," said Emily.

"We're getting paid, remember. Even if it's fun, it's work. We're just making work fun, that's all. I don't have a problem with that!"

That evening, they started looking over their samples.

Lisa started dissecting a Silver Carp. "Emily, check this out. Is this what I think it is?"

"What?"

"Look at this behind the gills."

"That looks like a tumor or something."

"No," said Lisa. " I think it's something else."

"Like what?"

"Think," said Lisa.

"You mean a suprabranchial organ?"

"Bingo," said Lisa.

"What the hell?"

"It is the start of a suprabranchial organ. It is beginning to develop."

"No way," stated Emily. "That's impossible."

"Yeah, well they are developing larger fins, too—so you know where I'm going with this?"

Lisa just looked at Emily, watching this new bit of information sink in. Lisa had never seen Emily look so concerned. Finally Emily spoke: "So, you're saying that you think they are developing a suprabranchial organ and will be able to breathe out of water? Breathe out of water? And they are getting these larger fins? Is this another one of your bad dreams?"

Lisa looked worried, too. "I'm flashing back to Chicago."

"I know, me too."

"No really, could it be?"

"Doesn't it make sense? It's all about food supply. They are evolving."

"But," said Lisa, "you know what this means?"

"Yeah," said Emily. "It means they could get up on land."

"Then what?"

"I don't know—one could eat your dog?"

"Or baby."

"Oh baby."

"I'm trying to think about the other fish with these," said Lisa.

"Well," said Emily, "there's the walking catfish."

"Yep, the Clarias batrachus."

"And the Snakehead."

"That one always gave me the creeps. I had a nightmare about the Channa argus."

"How about the Wooly Sculpin?"

"The Clinocottus analis? That one has a sexy name!"

"How about the Ell Catfish?"

"Yeah, the Channallabes apus."

"How about the Mexican Walking Fish?"

"Trick question. That's actually a salamander."

"Can't pull one over on you!"

"So," said Lisa, "all of those species also have larger pectoral fins. They use them to walk."

"And the carp are getting larger pectoral fins."

"And the suprabranchial organ."

"But it's happening too fast!"

"Tomorrow we write a report. The Shedd needs to get this information out to everyone. They will think we're crazy, though."

"We'll be the laughing stock of the aquarium probably," said Emily.

"We'll send them this sample. See what they say. It's just our hypothesis, that's all. Let's see what they think. We'll send them the report with the evidence as we see it."

"We'll scan the fish and send them the scan. We don't want to mail a dead carp—unless they ask for it."

"Please send us a dead carp," laughed Lisa. "Oh it feels better to laugh."

"We should just sleep on it tonight."

"Sleep on the dead carp?" laughed Lisa.

That evening they went online and checked out a home video showing mudpuppy behavior. Interestingly, they burrowed from shallow water to land, waiting there for an insect to come by. Their eyes were close to the top of their head and were all you could see as they lay in wait. Once the insect was spotted, they quickly crawled out of their burrow using their little arms and legs, pushing themselves along with their tail. They used their tail to lift themselves up, actually balancing on it.

The next day they wrote the report, scanned the fish and emailed the report to the Shedd. They decided to walk down to the state park. The boardwalk ended close to the ranger station but a concrete path continued along the river. There was a blue steel rail protecting pedestrians from the river on the one side of the path and large limestone landscape boulders on the other side. The path led past the campground to the pier projecting out into Lake Michigan. The pier was 1,650 feet long and had two lighthouses on it. One was a steel beacon about fifty feet tall and the other one was a tin-sided square house that sat up on a sloped concrete foundation to deflect large waves during storms. The light was held in a projection above the roof. The lighthouses were both painted bright red. A catwalk with lights on it connected both lighthouses to the land. Back before the lighthouses were automated, the keeper of the lights would use the catwalk during storms. In the worst weather, waves would wash over the pier. The catwalk kept the keeper of the lights safe.

The pier had lots of people walking on it. They would walk down to the end and watch the boats come in from the lake. There was one area where the teenagers jumped into the lake from the pier. People gathered around and watched all of the activities. From the pier there was also a great view of the beach with hundreds of people soaking up the sun.

"I'm hoping," said Lisa, "that this place never changes. It's so perfect."

"I know. But I keep thinking about these stupid ugly carp. They ruined the fishing industry already. That was big here."

"Let's walk down to the Bil-Mar and do a glass of wine on the patio—what a great view of Lake Michigan! We can watch the sunset there."

"Okay, let's walk down the wet sand and check out the bods—I've seen some pretty people."

"Who are you lookin' at most? The guys or the girls?" said Lisa.

"Oh, you know…I'm pretty non-discriminating."

"Doubles your chances of a date on a Saturday night!"

CHAPTER TEN
ROUGH DAY ON BEAVER ISLAND

The next morning, they were awakened by an urgent knock on the door. A coast guard officer was standing on the porch wearing a crisp white uniform. The uniform was tailored to his fit body. He looked about 40 years old.

"We got a call from the Shedd this morning. They told us about your findings. We also got a call from the guard on Beaver Island. They are having a problem there. It might all be related."

"What?" said Lisa, groggily.

"You're going on a plane ride today. Pack your bags and plan on spending the night. We leave in one hour. I'll send a guy to pick you up."

"What's so urgent?" asked Emily.

"I'll explain on the way. Get your bags packed. See you in an hour. Bring some hand nets," he stated as he pivoted on the porch.

"What is this all about?" asked Emily.

"I really don't know. He looked worried. He wouldn't say. We do get to go on a plane ride!"

"Yea, a plane ride. I like plane rides!" said Emily.

"How far is it?"

"A hundred sixty miles, I think. Probably take us a little more than an hour to get there."

They had just finished packing their bags as a coast guard vehicle rolled up in the driveway and beeped his horn twice.

"Well," said Emily. "I'm used to my dates coming up to the door to pick me up."

"I don't think it's that kind of date. We better get going."

They tossed their bags in the trunk and hopped into the back seat. After introducing themselves to the driver, they asked him what was going on.

"I have no information. I am just the taxi service today. I don't even get to go. All I know is that it's about someone getting killed. That's all I know."

"Killed?"

"Killed," he said.

He drove them the four miles to the local airport, past an industrial area. The buildings all had neatly kept lawns. Some of the industries had well-tended flower gardens. Driving through the gateway, he pulled up to the single engine Piper. The prop was rotating. They would be off in minutes.

"Watch the flap. Don't step on it," the pilot stated firmly as they approached the plane.

Lisa looked down at the wing. There was a sign: "Not A Step" on the flap.

"Okay, we got it," said Emily.

"Doesn't he think we can read?" whispered Lisa.

"He probably just doesn't want to have the plane fail. Pilots are fussy about that," whispered Emily back to Lisa.

"That's right, ladies," said the pilot.

"Wow, you have good hearing," said Lisa.

"One of you want to take the controls?" asked the pilot.

Emily and Lisa looked at each other. "You take the controls Emily, and I'm staying right here on the ground."

"Just kidding," said the pilot. "Ready for lift off. Oh, this is Kirk. He is the co-pilot. He'll take over if I have a heart attack."

"Good to see we all have a sense of humor," said Lisa.

He taxied the plane over to the runway and revved the engine. He called in and received clearance for take off. The small plane scooted down the runway and lifted into the air. It rocked as it started to climb, then became steady. He headed straight for the airspace above the beach, then radioed the Muskegon Airport to report his location. They would be flying close to the airport's controlled airspace, that airport being just a few miles inland from the coast. All planes by the water's edge needed to report.

He flew over the Grand Haven lighthouses and past the Grand River, then quickly passed the Muskegon Airport. Once past the airport, he came closer to the shoreline, following the beach, following it past the coastal cities of Pentwater, Ludington, Manistee, and Frankfort. Once past there, they could see the Grand Traverse Bay with the twenty-two mile long Old Mission Peninsula projecting out into it. The tip of the peninsula was just over the 45th parallel, about the same as Beaver Island. They were almost there.

Out in Lake Michigan on the left were the Manitou Islands. Soon they would see North and South Fox Islands, then Beaver Island surrounded on the west and north by a string of islands. They are Gull, High, Trout, Whiskey, Garden, and Hog Islands.

Beaver Island is the largest island in Lake Michigan. Besides the islands Emily and Lisa spotted from the plane, there were several smaller islands that completed the Beaver Island Archipelago. Thirteen miles long and anywhere between three and six miles wide, Beaver Island is positioned just above the 45th parallel. 45 degrees, 39 minutes North. A car ferry provides transportation there from Charlevoix, 32 miles away. Only 550 people live there year-round. As on most islands, people drive their cars to town and leave their keys in the ignition while shopping. If someone stole the car, how could it possibly disappear?

Landing at the main island airport—there are two airports—the plane was left running while Lisa and Emily grabbed their belongings and opened the door. "Watch the flap," reminded the pilot. "I'm going back to

Grand Haven. Have a good time. They'll call me when they want to have me pick you back up. See you in a month."

"A month!" said Lisa.

"Just kidding," said the pilot.

"Jeez," said Emily. "You're a riot!"

They got off from the plane and headed to a Suburban waiting for them. Inside the Suburban were two officers in the front and two young recruits in the third seat. They got into the center seat and introduced themselves.

"What's this all about?" inquired Lisa.

"Someone was attacked in Greenes' Bay—it's ten miles from here. We think that he was attacked in the water—that is where his body was found. There's not much left."

"Attacked by what?" asked Emily.

"A fish. Or lots of them. We don't know."

"I don't know about that," said Lisa. "We haven't heard of any fish attacks."

"Neither have we. This is a safe area. This was not done by a human, I'll tell you that. There's no bear or cougar or wolves on the island. It's small enough that an animal like that would be reported. We had some coyotes a few years ago but they disappeared. Some people didn't like them and we think that the coyotes got shot. There's some hermits on the island and they think there's no rules. I'll tell you this—there's one less hermit on the island now. The deceased was probably out wading, looking to spear a fish. This guy was known for that."

"What happened?" asked Emily.

"He got attacked. He always wore a fishing vest and had bobbers in the pockets for when he used a line. It's just his vest with a torso inside, that's it."

Emily and Lisa looked at each other. "We're not forensic scientists, you know. We don't know anything about this kind of stuff," said Lisa.

"Well," said the head officer. "You're going to find out about this stuff quick."

They drove down Fox Lake Road toward the bay, picking up West Side Road where Fox Lake Road ended. Within a few miles, they turned right on Greenes' Bay Road. They passed a small cabin with roll roofing on the roof and sides of the cabin. On the roof, the roofing was torn and peeled back in places. "That was his cabin there," said one of the recruits. "He lived large, huh?"

"Well," said Emily, "probably had no worries. Not caught up in the rat race. No mortgage, I bet the place wasn't insured, no heat bills—I see he had a fireplace—and what about electricity. Did he have that even?"

"Oil lamps. Off the grid. No gas, no electric, no septic system. He had an outhouse back there but that sort of collapsed and it was open air, but nobody's around anyway. Water he got from the lake. Hunted for his food. Rumor has it that he has a hundred grand in the bank here. He bought some vegetables in town during the summer. Probably spent a grand a year."

"Wouldn't that be nice. No bills. No bank to deal

with except to keep your money there. No car. No car insurance. No license. No cell phone."

"No cell phone! Are you kidding?" said Emily. "I can't live without my cell phone!!!!!"

"I don't think he was into texting, Emily," said Lisa.

"How you could live without texting, I don't know," said Emily.

"Apparently," said Lisa, "you can't."

They pulled up to the edge of the beach. There was a police cruiser waiting for them. Next to the cruiser was a stretcher with a small lump in the middle of it, covered with a white sheet. The Coast Guard officer provided the introductions.

"Are you ready for this?" asked the officer.

"We're biologists."

"We need your help," stated the officer.

He slowly removed the sheet. Beneath it was the torso. The canvas vest covered it well, but sticking out from the openings in the vest were the remnants of his neck and extremities. Lisa turned and vomited.

Emily covered her eyes as she choked down dry heaves.

Neither had seen a dead body before except for one well-prepared by a funeral home.

"Well!" said Emily. "I feel like I'm on a reality show and this is just a hoax."

"It's no hoax. We need your help. This is the deal. There are teeth marks everywhere and several teeth left in the victim. We needed to show you the damage first, now we will need to have you remove the teeth and identify them."

"Where's the cameras? I'm being set up, right?" said Emily.

"This is no joke."

"You remove the teeth. I'm not," said Emily.

"Very well," said the police officer. "From everything we've seen, there is no evidence that this death was caused by any individual or individuals. It is a crime of nature. We have combed the area and there is nothing here. He was attacked in the water. He was attacked by fish."

"There's been no record of any fish attacks anywhere. We've followed this from the beginning. People have gotten smacked by a flying fish but the fish haven't attacked. They were filter-feeders a year ago. They didn't eat anything but phytoplankton and zooplankton," said Emily.

"Things have changed, though," said Lisa.

"They couldn't have possibly changed this fast," said Emily.

"I don't know…look at the development of the suprabranchial organ."

"That's different."

"Is it? How is that so different?" asked Lisa. "We're talking about behavioral patterns now. Behavior patterns can change more quickly than genetics—look at how people behave. One minute they're fine, the next minute they're axe murderers. These fish have changed their genetics quickly, maybe now they're changing their behavior even more quickly. Okay then, pull those teeth out of the body—torso. Whatever. I can't stand to watch."

The officer took some eight inch long tweezers out of his patrol car. Usually they were used to remove bullets. He probed into the torso and collected several teeth. "How many do you need? There's lots of them in here."

"Six. Eight. Whatever," said Emily.

He removed the teeth and put them in a baggie. "Look," he said. "I'll give them a rinse with peroxide, if you'd like, unless that would damage the DNA or something. There's other ones in here anyways, so there's other samples. Do you want me to clean them?"

"Clean them," said Emily and Lisa in unison.

He went back to the patrol car and poured peroxide into the baggie and shook it around. Then he went to the water's edge and rinsed the bag. Pouring the teeth into his hand, he did a final rub to remove bits of flesh, then handed the teeth to Emily.

Lisa looked the teeth over. "Jeez," she said. "Boy, do these look familiar."

Emily looked at Lisa. "This can't possibly be happening," said Emily.

"We'll take these with us," said Lisa. "We'll have info for you tomorrow."

The coast guard personnel and Lisa and Emily went back to the Suburban, leaving the cop there with the torso. He had already called the one connection he had on the island to arrange for a coroner on the mainland to pick up the torso. The coroner would take the Beaver Islander, the ferry, to the island the next morning.

In the cop's mind, the investigation was over. The hermit had been mauled by some fish. He would take the torso back to his small office and wrap it in plastic and put it in the freezer. He had a dog's head in there, too, waiting to be picked up by the health department. It needed to be tested for rabies.

The Suburban went back to Greenes' Bay Road and turned left on West Side Road, then continued straight on Hannigan's Road. "We'll take East Side Road back toward town just to show you a different part of the island," said the officer. "Beautiful place, isn't it–very peaceful."

"Yep," said Lisa, "except for the occasional murder."

One of the recruits piped in: "You know what I think—I think the cop's right. That body wasn't cut up—it was chewed up. Nobody could do that to a body."

"And the teeth," said the other recruit.

"We'll see about those," said Emily. "Let's not jump to conclusions."

The Suburban turned on East Side Road, which ran right up the coast. "There's the CMU Biological Station," the officer pointed out. "We'll be calling them and you'll have access to their lab."

"That's Central Michigan University, right?" asked Lisa.

"Yep, it's over in Mt. Pleasant."

"Are there mountains in the middle of Michigan?" asked Emily.

The officers and recruits laughed. "Nah. But I heard about a girl from Spain who decided to go there because she wanted to be close to the mountains. Boy was she surprised! Pretty much flat as a pancake."

"One thing I like about this island," said Emily, "is that the roads all have sensible names. West Side Road is on the west side, this is East Side Road on the east side, Fox Lake Road led to Fox Lake, Greenes' Bay Road led to Greenes' Bay."

They continued past King's Highway and the road changed names and became Darkeytown Road.

"Darkeytown Road!" said Emily. "That's not PC."

"Been like that forever, but it's being changed now," said the officer.

One of the recruits spoke up. "It originally was 'Darkey Mike's Road.' It eventually got renamed to 'Darkeytown Road.' It should have stayed 'Darkey Mike's Road.' It sounds better. Darkey Mike was maybe five generations ago. He was Irish, like lots of us here. There's a recessive gene in the Irish and sometimes someone comes out with a darker complexion, like there's anything wrong with that! So he had a darker complexion and that was his nickname, so what! And he did a lot for the island, so the road was named after him. He didn't name himself that, but that was his nickname. Probably hated it at first. But he did so much for the island, they named the road after him. Things have changed."

Another recruit spoke: "They had a town meeting, most attended, I hear. People were outside the town hall yelling in the open windows because there wasn't enough room inside for them to attend the hearing. People didn't want the name changed, just to be PC. 'This is what it's been, this is what it should stay,' they yelled. Especially his rels. Why take it away from him? Just because he had a darker complexion and that was his nickname? There is a road named after him. Leave it be!!! Almost racist to remove the name because he had a darker complexion and had a road named after him!"

"But," said the driver, "new people who lived on the road didn't like giving their address as 'Darkeytown Road.' It was embarrassing, I guess. So they lobbied for the change. It was debated and is being changed to 'Barney's Lake Road.' But, 'Darkeytown Road' is still the name locals use. Like when the Smiths buy the Jones' house and live there for thirty years. It still will be the Jones' house."

"911 wanted a single name to respond to. Not that we have many emergencies here, but they wanted a single name, so it's being changed to 'Barney's Lake Road' on the maps, but they're still going to put 'Darkeytown Road' on the maps as 'formerly,'" he said.

Lisa spoke up. "On an island, perhaps it would be possible to unite and to exist as a singular unit, since the island is small. Even though newcomers arrive, which is necessary and inevitable, everybody should be able to get along. I guess it's not that big of a deal. As long as you understand the history of the name, it's no big deal."

"You know," said Emily, "someday everyone might accept these things as history and they will have real meaning. Changing things just to be PC may not be the way to go."

"People are most worried about not being viewed as PC," said Lisa.

"Well," said Emily, "then they should worry more about themselves."

"I just thought I'd show you the upper west side of the island," said the officer, changing the subject. "It has the second largest lake on the island, Font Lake, and is the most inhabited. You're going to stay up by the DNR office."

"Where's that?" asked Lisa.

"Right up on the top east side of the island. If you ever get lost, just ask someone where Sucker Point is and they'll point you toward your new home."

"Sucker Point. Couldn't have they come up with something just a bit more…more…well, anything but 'Sucker Point'!" said Lisa.

The little downtown area of St. James had a few restaurants and hotels and was within walking distance of Sucker Point. "Where's the local watering hole?" asked Lisa. "I think I need a drink."

"You probably want to go to Earl's Joint. It's not too classy of a place," said the officer.

"Ha. You don't think we're classy?" asked Emily.

"Sorry, that didn't come out right," said the officer. "I just meant that you don't probably need white linens right now."

"Really," said Emily, "I don't think I'm going to eat for a week."

"Well, we sort of get used to it after a while—fishing bodies out of the water—not too pretty sometimes, especially the ones that don't go floating for a few months. Can't even tell if it's a guy or girl, young or old, nothing. Sometimes the flesh just peels off the bones like overcooked chicken," said the officer.

"Oh good," said Emily. "Now I won't be able to eat chicken again."

"Sorry," said the officer. "TMI."

"Yeah," said Emily looking at Lisa. "Too much information alright!"

The officer dropped them off at the bar and they made plans to hook up the next day. "We'll need some time to figure this out," said Lisa, entering his number in her phone. "I'll give you a call tomorrow when we have something."

They went into the bar. "Pitchers. What draft in pitchers do you have?"

"Just the two of you?" asked the waiter.

"Yep," said Lisa. "We've had a hard day."

"Anything you want to share?" asked the waiter with a grin.

"No," said Emily. "Just a rough day on Beaver Island."

LAKESHARK! INVASION OF THE ASIAN CARP

CHAPTER ELEVEN
OFFICER MCFADDEN

That evening they stayed at the Sunrise Motel. They spread the teeth out on the desk and focused the gooseneck lamp onto the specimens. With a pencil they found in the drawer below, they moved the teeth around on the desktop, looking at every side of each of the teeth, studying them.

"I don't know what to say, Lisa, but these sure do look like the samples we got from the Silver Carp a month ago. Remember, they were round and pointy like these—like puppy teeth—a little smaller, the same color…I can't wait to get these under a microscope. The carp's teeth are sure beginning to look like the teeth from that guy Nate who wanted to date me in high school."

"I don't know—even some sheephead have better teeth than lots of guys who used to ask me out," said Lisa. "Sheephead teeth sure look human. Ever go out with Nate?"

"Yeah, after he got braces," said Emily.

"Look, at this tooth."

"That one is a little different," said Emily.

"Maybe from another fish—two fish?"

"They're like pike teeth maybe. Bigger in the front and rows of teeth that get progressively smaller as they recess back into the mouth."

"In a pike, the lingual area of the gumline has hundreds of pin-sized teeth."

"All teeth start small."

"So these could be from a more mature fish or it could be that our other specimens were from the rear of the mouth—they could lose those first."

"These are bigger. The largest we've seen from a possible carp."

"Well, what else could they be from?" asked Emily.

"Well, maybe a pike, but I'm not convinced that a pike or a carp could do this at all." said Lisa.

"Okay, but then how did the teeth get in that body? Tell me that."

"Some guy murdered the hermit and stuck them in there to throw off the investigation. I saw a CSI episode like that," said Lisa

"Did CSI catch their man?"

"At 8:57."

"Hope we're that lucky! I've not felt that lucky lately," said Emily.

"Let's see what happens."

"Let's drink another beer," said Lisa.

They wound down the evening and decided to go to the lab in the morning.

The next morning they rented some mopeds and took their samples down to the CMU lab. They studied the teeth removed from the torso next to teeth they had removed from carp samples. They closely matched those of the jumping Silver Carp. "Okay then," said Emily. "So they seem to be from the Silver, but that still doesn't mean that the fish did all that damage. I'm not convinced about that."

"Let's moped around the island and paw this over. Maybe go back to Greenes' Bay. Wade around in the water some. See what we can find," said Lisa.

"Okay. Let's tell the cop what we're doing. Stop by his office first. Wow! I don't even know his name!"

"Me neither, but I don't think there's many cops on this island. With that torso there, I wasn't exactly into pleasantries."

"We should let him know our findings, too—preliminary findings—just so he knows. And, let's have the coroner remove the rest of the teeth. I'm sure he would appreciate the work!" said Emily. "We may need them, who knows?"

The biologists went to the police station and met up with the cop. His name was Paul McFadden. He grew up on the island, went to Northern Michigan University, taking Criminal Justice courses and returned to the island as its sole police officer. His great grandfather had been one of the settlers on the island and they named a point on the west side of the island "McFadden Point." It was just north of Greenes' Bay.

They told Officer McFadden about their findings and informed him about their day's plans.

"Be careful," he warned. "Anything can happen."

Lisa and Emily turned and walked out the door. As they walked down the wooden steps and into the street, they heard the officer's phone ring. The officer came running out the door. "Ladies! Hold up for a minute!"

He finished his conversation and hung up the phone. "There's trouble."

He grabbed a shotgun off from the rack behind his desk. "Come with me. We're going to Indian Point. It's right up on the north side of the island."

"What's up?" asked Lisa.

"Sounds like another fish attack!"

"Wait a minute," said Emily. "We're not even sure about the first one yet."

"Buckle up, we're going for a ride," he said.

"I get shotgun," said Emily. "You ride in the back like a prisoner," she told Lisa.

"Bitch!" said Lisa.

McFadden put his gun in the trunk and hopped into the driver's seat. He stepped on the gas and peeled out as he left the station.

"Just like the movies," said Emily.

"We just do that to impress the crowd," said McFadden. "Took a class on peeling out at Northern. 'Peeling out, 101.'"

"How far to the point?" asked Lisa.

"Three miles," he said.

"Someone got bit?" asked Lisa.

"Dead." That's all he said.

Emily and Lisa rode in silence as they raced toward the point. They both were holding on tightly to the door handles. McFadden knew how to drive and he knew every turn and every bump in the road. He probably could have done it with his eyes closed.

He slowed down and pulled into a small parking lot. "Well, if the police work doesn't work out for you, you could always be a New York cabbie," joked Lisa.

"Always drove fast. One of the reasons I like being a cop. What are they going to do–give me a ticket? Let's go."

They ran toward the beach where there was a crowd gathered. Still in the water, but at the very edge, was a young girl about fourteen years old. She was obviously dead and was missing both legs. Sixteen people formed a circle around her. Other adults were keeping the children away.

"Who knows what happened?" questioned McFadden to the crowd.

One person spoke up. "I was standing right here watching the waves, just enjoying the morning. There were some kids out in the water–not too deep–maybe four feet deep. I could see her bikini top–she was away from the group just a bit, maybe twenty feet away. I saw a fin sticking out of the water. I looked again and I couldn't believe it. Then the fin came closer to her and she started screaming. The other kids started screaming, too. Some came running in toward the beach. Some tried to run toward her, but it happened so fast. Suddenly she started to go under, like her legs buckled, but now I realize she was getting her legs eaten off. It happened so fast, then it was over and two boys grabbed her arms and pulled her body in. We couldn't believe it!"

Lisa and Emily looked at each other, then at the body. The victim had long wavy dark hair and beautiful features.

"Fin?" asked Emily. "Like what kind of fin?"

"Like a little shark fin. Like in the movies, but smaller. Just like in the movies. I thought it was a joke or something at first, but her screams. I knew it was real," said the one witness.

"How long did the attack, the alleged attack, take?" asked Lisa.

"Alleged!? Does this look alleged? She was attacked! She doesn't have any legs!"

"Okay, well how long, then?"

"Two minutes tops. Then she was done for. It happened just like that."

Emily looked at the cop. "I think we should get her out of here. Isn't there somewhere we can take her? We need to probe for more teeth…or at least you do."

"There's a little clinic in town. I'll call the doc. He'll help us out."

All the cop had in his car was a blanket. He retrieved it and laid it on the ground, then lifted the body onto it and wrapped the victim up. Her name, they found out, was Teresa. Her femurs protruded from her flesh, sticking out at least six inches. Ribbons of flesh hung from the severed limbs.

They took her to the local doctor's office and got a cart they could put the body on. Wheeling the body inside, McFadden warned the doctor that it was grizzly.

"Seen it all," said the doc. "Seen it all. Should have been there with me in Korea. Yep, some awful stuff there. Was a medic, you know that. Seen it all."

Once inside, they placed the body on a stainless steel table with an inch and a half lip around all sides. This was to keep fluids from running off. "Got this from the coroner. Used it for the autopsies. Nice solid table. Say, I should call him. You got another one, I heard."

"Yep," said McFadden. "Hermit Greene."

"Oh no," said the doc.

"Yep."

"The coroner is coming in this afternoon on the boat. Guess we should tell him to be ready for two. You got to be better at this than me, Doc. Could you see if you can find some fish teeth buried in what's left of her legs?"

"Fish teeth?" said the doctor. "You think a fish did this? Never heard of that. Been 'round a long time, too. Lived here back before the war–you know that–seen it all but never seen this on this island, no, never seen this, never seen this," he continued as he probed into the torn flesh. "Never seen this."

"Here," the doctor said. "This what you're lookin' for?"

He showed the tooth to Lisa. "That's what we're lookin' for," she said. "We would like to have as many samples as possible. We need to compare them with samples we took from some other fish. Match 'em up. See if this could possibly be happening. It seems unexplainable," she said.

"Well," said the doctor. "I'll find as many as there are in there. I'll give you the teeth, you do the explaining."

The doctor found twenty teeth embedded in the torn flesh. He looked over the rest of the body. There were no tooth marks anywhere else. Whatever had done this had focused only on the legs, unlike how the hermit had been mauled. There had been less time, apparently. With the other people around, maybe it was just a hit and run attack. "Beautiful girl," said the doctor. "Too bad."

McFadden sent out an alert to everyone on the island: "Swim at your own risk. We are advising you not to swim." Lisa and Emily contacted the Shedd. "Let's err on the side of caution," they said, "and warn everybody that the water in and around Lake Michigan may not be safe for swimming."

Emily and Lisa took the salvaged teeth over to the CMU lab and compared them to the samples they had brought over to the island. Under the microscope, they looked virtually identical. "But," said Lisa, "a tooth is not a fingerprint." Many species have teeth that look similar to another's. I'm not jumping to any conclusions. We need to keep an open mind."

"But," said Emily, "something is happening here."

"Something's happening, alright. Look at that computer. Check out our telemetry—there's no tagged carp anywhere. They disappeared."

"It only works to 200 feet deep. How deep is Lake Michigan?"

"Nine hundred twenty-three is the maximum depth."

"Pretty much directly west of here—that's where the hole is, right?"

"Yep. Just below the 45th parallel. I looked at the bathymetry charts the other day," said Lisa.

"Haven't you been busy."

"Maybe they're schooling down there."

"Chillin'."

"Chillin' down in the hole."

The next day they rented the mopeds and rode around the perimeter, stopping at any access point they could, wading out into the water looking for anything out of the ordinary. Everything was still. They saw nothing. The water, it seemed, was totally devoid of any form of life. Whereas typically there would be schools of minnows in shallow water, today there were none. Wherever they investigated, they found the same thing—nothing.

That evening, they decided that they would rent kayaks and paddle around the entire island. It would take two days. Beaver Island's perimeter is over 44 miles around, depending on the water level of Lake Michigan.

"I was all hyped up for the trip down the Grand River," Emily said. "And it never came to fruition."

"Well," said Lisa, "we got a bit sidetracked. When the coast guard officer knocked on our door that morning, everything changed."

They borrowed a tent, some sleeping bags, a cooler, and cooking gear from McFadden, telling him about their plans and when to expect their return in two days. He told them to camp on the Charlevoix school property—he'd clear it for them. It was on Nicksau's Point and there was no way you could miss the location: it also was the home of the Beaver Head Light. "Even if you're out until dark, just aim for the lighthouse," he said. It was exactly half way around the island from their starting point at the top of the island. "But," he added, "I think you should be off the water before dark."

They bought some food at Frank's Butcher Shop, along with some ice, loaded the cooler and drove down to the southern tip of the island. After pitching the tent on the school property and leaving their cooler and cooking gear, Lisa and Emily drove back up to the launch. The Shamrock Restaurant had a lunch special that day, so they ate lunch and packed some snacks before starting the trip. It was decided that they would go clockwise around the island.

The water on the east side of the island was substantially shallower until you were far from shore, so they ventured out from shore to reach deeper water. The clarity of the water was amazing. They were aware, of course, that the water around the Chicago area was more turbid, however they didn't think that there normally was such a difference.

"You know," said Lisa, "that the phytoplankton and zooplankton have diminished so much in this entire lake that now the water is almost absolutely pure. It's been filtered by these carp and there's nothing left for the species on the low end of the food chain anymore."

"I know," said Emily, "it's like the water's been filtered by reverse osmosis or something. There's other lakes in Michigan that I've heard of that are very, very clear—what is it—that one we read about in Beulah?

"Crystal Lake, duh."

"There's no fish in it either. So is that what Lake Michigan is going to be like?"

"Except for the occasional carp."

"Things come back—look at Lake Erie—you studied that, right?"

"Oh yeah, that's a good one. The 'dead lake' they called it. Thought it would take a hundred years for life to come back into it."

"Came back in twenty years or something, right?"

"Yep. Good walleye in there now."

"That's a shallow one—I wonder if that helped it."

"No one knows. Everybody was surprised."

"We need to take samples of the water here and see if there's anything in it," said Lisa.

"CMU might have the equipment we need. Let's ask them tomorrow."

"Measure the phytoplankton and zooplankton in the water—what's your guess on how many in a cubic foot?" asked Emily.

"Maybe ten thousand."

"Wow. That's nothing!"

"I know," said Lisa, "that's how pure it looks. What's your guess?"

"Ten thousand and one."

"Bitch! You can't do that. This isn't 'The Price Is Right.'"

"Okay then, twenty thousand."

"That's better."

"Hey, look at that," said Emily.

"What?"

"Look over there. What is that?"

Lisa looked out into the open water in the direction Emily was pointing. There was a dark spot on the water about a hundred yards out from where they sat in their kayaks. It was moving slowly, moving parallel to shore. "Tell me that's not a fin," said Lisa. It looked like it stuck up just five inches from the surface of the water.

"Why didn't we bring the binocs," said Emily.

"That would have been smart."

"I think it's coming closer," said Emily.

"What the hell is it?"

"Man, it is a fin!"

"Don't move," cautioned Lisa.

"Get your paddle out of the water, too," said Emily.

They both sat there quietly in their kayaks and watched as the object came towards them. By now they could see that it definitely was a fin. As it got closer, they could see that the fin actually protruded more than five inches from the water. The giant fish moved slowly. Lisa and Emily were twenty feet from each other. "If anything happens," said Lisa, "I love you."

"Love you too."

"Don't talk," cautioned Lisa.

They sat there watching this fin come directly toward them. When the fish was forty feet away, they could see its outline. It was a Silver Carp. It was over twenty feet long. They watched as it swam right between their kayaks. They sat motionless. The fish kept swimming toward shore, then turned and followed the shoreline. When it was out of sight, Lisa and Emily looked at each other.

"Ready?" asked Lisa.

"Don't splash too much, paddle quietly. If there's any more of those around here, we don't want them to start jumping around us."

They paddled directly to shore, beached the kayaks, and started walking toward the nearest road. They were by Point LaPar, about eight miles from town.

"Terra firma," said Emily.

"Never thought I'd be so glad to be on land."

"I'm shaking," said Emily.

"That's nothing," said Lisa. "I peed my pants!"

"Now what?"

"Let's get back to the motel, think this through. We have some calls to make in the morning."

"Hey, I was looking forward to camping out tonight," said Emily.

"First of all, I need to change into some dry pants. That freaked me out terribly," said Lisa.

"Well, we can pick up the stuff in the morning. So much for camping."

"We have a motel rented. Might as well use it. Anything on TV tonight?" asked Lisa.

"I think it's shark week. We could watch that," she said with a grin.

"I think our work here is done. Let's skedaddle to the mainland tomorrow and get back to Grand Haven," said Emily. "This 'event' or whatever you want to call it is not going to be privy to only Beaver Island. We need to alert everybody all around the lake—and rivers. These fish are monsters. Anything could happen. Anything," said Emily.

"We'll call for the plane when we get back to the motel."

"How about the water samples?" asked Emily.

"We'll have CMU take some. See what the students come up with."

"How far are we from the motel?" asked Emily.

"Seven, eight miles maybe."

"You ever hitchhike?"

"No. Are you kidding. There're crazy people out there!"

"My dad always said that," said Emily. "But we're on the island. Nothing but nice here."

"Yeah. It'll be fun to hitch a ride."

Once they found the road, the first car that they saw picked them up and gave them a ride directly to their motel.

That night, they bought a bottle of Old Crow whiskey and walked down to Whiskey Point. They needed to chill.

The next day they met the pilot at the same airport and made a special request—they wanted to be taken on an air tour over the entire archipelago. They wanted to fly low to see if they could spot any of the large fish.

"Just think," said Emily. "We could be doing this in our kayaks!"

"Just think," responded Lisa, "we could end up like the hermit!"

"Don't get me wrong, I'll investigate whatever needs to be investigated any way I can," said Emily.

"This is prudent. I'm not wussing out."

"Let's just say we're covering more ground this way," said Emily.

"Water," corrected Lisa.

The plane circled all of the neighboring islands. They could not see anything out of the ordinary.

"They must all be in the deep water," said Emily.

After spending over an hour searching, they bee-lined back to Grand Haven.

CHAPTER TWELVE
BACK IN GRAND HAVEN

Once they got back to the ranger station, Emily texted the group of six people they had met to see if they wanted to get together that evening. She received a text back that said "8." This gave Lisa and Emily a little time to walk down to the lighthouse and do a little people-watching.

The surf had kicked up quite a bit and there were several people on their boards waiting to catch a wave. Teenagers were still jumping off from the pier—technically a no-no—but a routine event anyway. Kids had broken their ankles there, hitting large boulders buffeting up the pier. There existed only a very limited area to land in. And, even in that area, one needed to keep from going too deep. The neophytes were the ones that usually hurt themselves. There was also the danger of not clearing the lower retainer while jumping. The danger, and the prohibition, made it fun.

Parents were taking pictures of their children down at the end of the pier, waiting until a large wave splashed up against the pier's wall, offering a dynamic backdrop. Several boats were returning from the day on the lake while others were on their way out to watch the sunset.

Back in the day, there would be many boats going out at this time to do some fishing. The die-hard fishermen now went to the inland lakes where there were still some panfish. It wasn't like the good ol' days when it came to fishing.

Later Lisa and Emily walked back to the ranger station and took long showers. They put on some nicer clothes, being tired of living out of suitcases for the last few days.

When their friends came over, they decided to buy several bottles of wine and walk down to the beach and wait for the sunset. The sun wouldn't set for an hour, but the prelude to the sunset was sometimes the best part.

This evening, though, the best part was after the sunset. The sky turned lavender and orange, with streaks of color running from the horizon line in the west to high up in the sky. Purplish jet-streams added to the drama. They polished off the three bottles of Chardonnay and decided to go down to the Kirby to see if there was anything going on there. There were just a few people in the downstairs bar, so they went upstairs to shoot some pool. There were five bar-size seven foot tables in good condition. They took two tables and played cut-throat.

Rum and coke ended up being the drink of the night, so after the pool games became sloppy, they walked back down to the ranger station. Emily and Lisa started talking about what they had experienced over on Beaver Island.

"The carp, it seems," explained Lisa, "are definitely growing—tell them about the one we saw kayaking."

"Carps kayaking," laughed Joe.

"Ha. Yeah. You know what I meant!"

"When I see a kayaking carp, I'll believe both of you about their advancements!" said Joe.

"It was big," said Emily. "Twenty feet."

"Stay out of the water, seriously," said Lisa.

"A girl got her legs eaten off."

"I hardly believe it," said Ramsey. "There's no freshwater fish that big—not even a sturgeon."

"You're right about that," said Emily. "I studied sturgeon in college."

"I saw it with my own eyes," said Lisa. "I peed my pants!"

Everybody laughed. "I'm serious. I peed my pants!!!"

"Still," said Ramsey, "maybe the water magnified it."

"Were you guys smoking weed or something?" asked Gina as she twirled her hair.

"Maybe Beaver Island has a Bermuda Triangle," said Betty.

"Maybe it was an alien," said Gina.

"They haven't been around here, that's for sure. We haven't seen any big fish and we've been out on the cig hull," stated Ramsey.

"Well, Joe, you've been a little quiet over there—what do you think?" asked Paul.

"I could run a computer model. I can figure anything out on the computer!" he said.

"He can, too," said Betty. "The idiot even wrote a program on how much weight I'd gain if I kept on gaining like I did the freshman year. He came up with 850 pounds. So I gained the 'Freshman fifteen,' well he didn't have to rub it in. He figured that I had a good seventy more years to live—you know, to 90—then 70 x 15 was a thousand or something but he deducted for getting older and not gaining so much, you know, when you're 80, and then he added on my 120 pounds now and came up with 850. I told him no way was I going to weigh 850."

"I say no way you're 120," said Cassandra. "I weigh 120 and I'm two feet taller than you."

"You're not two feet taller than me."

"Girls, girls…I just did it as a joke," said Joe. "I was kidding her."

"About her weight?" said Gina. "You can't kid a girl about her weight!"

"I'm young and stupid," said Joe. "She took it personally."

"Well yeah, I took it personally—you're lucky I'm still hanging with you," said Betty.

"It was a mistake," said Joe. "I learn from my mistakes. Besides, I think my math was off. You're really going to weigh 1,000."

Betty jumped on Joe and started pounding on him.

"I'm kidding. I'm kidding," Joe kept on saying. "It was a joke."

"That dude's gonna have to get a better sense of humor," said Cassandra. "He may not survive."

Paul pulled Betty off from Joe. "Come on now, he's just trying to be an asshole."

"He's good at that," said Ramsey. "He really don't have to try."

Everybody settled down and the topic got back to the fish. "Stay outta the water," cautioned Emily. "I'm serious."

"I'm thinking we should take the boat over there and just check it out. We don't have to go swimming or nothing," said Paul.

"Don't do it," said Lisa.

"How far is it?" asked Betty, still hyperventilating from her attack.

"One hundred sixty miles," said Emily.

"A lot of fuel," said Ramsey. "If we take it slow, which we never do, four MPG—what is that, Joe?"

"Forty gallons, each way. Three hundred bucks."

"Round trip?" asked Ramsey.

"Yes," answered Joe patiently. "Three hundred round trip."

"That ain't bad," said Ramsey. "I'm not afraid. I'm gonna be a cop!"

"Yeah, we met a nice cop up there," said Lisa. "McFadden. Officer McFadden. Nice guy. Really knew how to drive!"

"Bad ass," said Emily. "Scared the hell out of us!"

"Where'd he go to school—you know?" asked Ramsey.

"Northern."

"Oh yeah, they have a good school. Show you how to drive on snow 'cause that's all they have up there."

"That's in the Upper Peninsula, right?" asked Cassandra.

"No," said Gina. "I heard it was in the UP."

"The UP is the Upper Peninsula, dear," said Paul.

"Oh yeah," said Gina. "I knew that."

"Well, I'd still say don't go to Beaver Island. We're staying away for now." said Lisa.

"From what the eyewitnesses said, it definitely was a fish," said Emily. "We cautioned everybody to stay out of the water."

"What's the fish gonna do—eat our boat?" laughed Ramsey.

"We have no idea. We just don't want anybody to get hurt. It ain't pretty."

"Oh yeah, what'd it look like?" asked Paul.

"You don't want to know," said Lisa. "You really don't want to know."

"I could take it," said Ramsey. "I'm gonna be a cop."

"We know that already," said Paul. "And I'm gonna be a gym teacher, but I don't go around telling everyone all the time."

"And me," said Joe. "I'm going into stand up comedy."

"You better work on your act," said Betty. "I'll heckle you off stage!"

"Maybe you will be his act," chided Cassandra. "He can tell fat jokes."

With that, Betty flung herself at Cassandra. She wasn't trying to hurt her, she just didn't want to let her get away with the comment.

"Catfight!!!" everybody yelled. They let Betty and Cassandra wrestle around for a while and everybody clapped and yelled their approval. "It's like 'Beauty and the Beast,'" said Paul.

The girls stopped wrestling and looked at each other. Simultaneously, they leapt on Paul and started hitting him as hard as they could. Paul just laughed and covered his head and his balls.

"Who's the beast, idiot?" they yelled.

"Cover your balls most, Paul," said Joe. "They're more important than your head."

"Let's get him girls. Come on Gina. Join the fun." All three girls leapt on Paul, along with Joe. "Hell," said Ramsey. "I feel left out." Ramsey leapt on Paul, too, and they had a good match.

CHAPTER THIRTEEN
THE CIGARETTE HULL BOAT TRIP

Two days later, against Emily and Lisa's warnings, the three couples prepared to launch the cigarette hull boat at the Pigeon Lake launch and head to Beaver Island. The beauty of this launch was that you could get to Lake Michigan about as quick as possible. Other launches had long "no wake" zones. It was difficult to hold the cigarette hull boat back, idling for forty-five minutes or so as the boat navigated through the no wake zones. But, if you went too fast, there would probably be a meeting with the Coast Guard, or the sheriff. They needed to avoid these problems. Paul and Gina, the future gym and kindergarten teachers, would sit in the rear seat. Joe, the computer guy, and Betty, the future English teacher, would take the center seat. Ramsey, the future cop, and Cassandra, the volleyball player, would take turns driving the boat.

In the early evening the day before, Ramsey had everybody get their stuff together so that there would be no delay leaving. The larger the crowd, the slower the movement. He had his friends load their stuff in the boat the night before.

They packed enough food and beer, as well as dope, to make the trip. Everybody brought raincoats to prepare for any type of weather, but a limited amount of clothing. Lake Michigan could get rough at the drop of a hat, so it was wise to be prepared. It was smart to bring raincoats. Basically, though, they hoped to be wearing swimsuits and not much else.

The friends chipped in to fill the boat up with 100 gallons of fuel at the local on-land gas station. This topped off the fuel tanks. They knew that the gas would be more expensive at marinas on the way. The thing was, once on the water they didn't want to stop anywhere. There were marinas here and there, but they were just a bit out of the way. They wanted to bee-line over to Beaver Island.

Ramsey checked the oil levels in both of the engines and made sure that the lower drives had plenty of oil. He double-checked to make sure he had at least two extra quarts of lower drive oil with him packed in a mesh bag down in the engine compartment—an emergency stash. He always carried the cover for the boat to button it up during inclement weather. He went over his mental check-list. Once out on the big lake, there was little that could be done if something was missing. Ramsey always compared it to backpacking: you didn't want to take too much but you had to take everything that would be needed. "Not too much, everything needed," was his mantra.

There were always some basics on the boat: flashlights and batteries, first-aid kit, aspirin, sea-sickness pills, rain ponchos, sunscreen, water, and emergency food rations. The boat was required to have life preservers, a toss-ring, flares, a loud blast-horn, and fire extinguishers. There was also an inflatable life raft and an inner tube that was always kept on board, not required but prudent. Ramsey went over his mental checklist. "Got it," he said to nobody in particular when he was sure that nothing else was needed. "I believe we are ready to go."

The next morning, awaking at 5 A.M., they got up, took quick showers, and headed off to the launch. Ramsey backed the trailered boat into the water beside the dock. Paul and Joe released it from the trailer. Cassandra, Betty, and Gina each grabbed a mooring rope to secure it to the dock while Ramsey parked the truck and trailer. There was plenty of parking in the lot. Back when fishing was big, the launch would have been packed. There were weekends when parking overflowed onto the shoulder of the road.

Starting the engines, Ramsey asked everyone whether they had everything. "It's now or never," he said. "Once we're on the lake we're on the lake." Everybody thought about it for a second and confirmed that they were prepared. "Aye, aye, captain," said Paul.

Ramsey backed the long boat out away from the docks and kept it in reverse for the first 150 feet. It was a tight harbor with shallows on both sides. Lily pads and cattails identified the shallow water—as well as buoys could ever possibly have. Ramsey kept the props tilted almost all the way up as he maneuvered the boat away from the launch. When he was far enough out into the water, he lowered the props some and began to spin the boat around. "We have to stay to the right at first until we get past those weeds, then we have to work our way over toward those docks on the other side of the lake," he told Cassandra. "Then we stay near the docks, go through the channel, and we're home free."

Pigeon Lake is shallow, so shallow that it is hard to circle around the lake. Larger boats, such as this one, navigate through the lake with the captain always looking at the depth meter. It suddenly gets shallow in spots. Ramsey was careful and didn't lower his props all the way until he passed through the gooseneck separating the lake from the channel. Piers went out into Lake Michigan 600 feet, helping boats to reach deep water. Without the piers, the bottom of the lake would have to be dredged weekly. As it was, dredging was done at least once a year. Sand was extracted from the bottom of the channel and pumped into the shallow water by the nearby beach.

The rumbling of the twin 454's resounded from the steel piling of the piers as Ramsey navigated through the channel. "See," said Ramsey once he could see the lake past the piers, "the lake is smooth!" Lake Michigan had waves just six inches to one foot high, about as smooth as ever. This would make for an easy trip. There was nothing worse than powering through large swells, pounding through the large swells. It was the difference between driving a car down a washboard road verses driving a car down a newly-paved asphalt road. This seemed to be ideal. Ramsey knew that the conditions could change—conditions were always changing. He had checked out the forecast, of course, and had found out that all predictions were positive.

There were times when boats should not be taken out on the lake. Storms can come up fast. Most of the storms were predictable; some were not. Today's forecast and the next day's called for a maximum of two-and-a-half foot waves, about as good as it ever gets. "Are we ready!" shouted Ramsey over the twin 454's. "Hang on to your hats!" He was almost at the end of the piers as he throttled the boat up a bit and started his turn into the lake. Once past the piers he shoved the throttle forward and the boat quickly came into plane. The bow settled down and Ramsey backed off the throttle some to set a cruising speed of twenty five miles per hour. It was about as slow as the boat would go while still achieving plane. "Feel okay?" asked Ramsey, smiling at Cassandra. "Any slower and the bow will come up and start pushing water. The boat will use more fuel. See how I can back off the throttle once the bow comes down and we're on plane? When we're on plane, a minimum amount of the boat is in the water—it is just gliding over the surface."

"It feels so smooth," replied Cassandra. "I like this speed."

"Great!"

"Remember that one time you went balls-out up by Pentwater? Oh man that was fun but it was hard on the body, too. The boat was leaping out of the water!" said Cassandra.

"It was rough that day," said Ramsey. "We could go balls-out today and it would be okay, in fact we will after a while just for the hell of it. Not for long, just to blow the boat out for a bit. The engines are like wild horses—they need to get out and run a bit. Like nine hundred and eight wild horses," he said, referring to the twin 454's.

In the early morning the lake is usually smoother than later in the day. Getting to bed early and getting up early was prudent. The sky was just beginning to lighten. It would be an hour or more before they would see the sun—the barrier dune along the coast increased the height of the horizon line. These dunes raised dramatically from the water's edge, loaded with hardwoods and pines. The oldest trees poked up from the horizon line, standing tall and proud, rightfully so after having weathered their one hundred plus years of often harsh weather. The sky was totally clear to the west—the direction the weather typically came from—so Ramsey felt confident. In the east there were wispy clouds orange and backlit by the rising sun. The moon had not set yet, over half full. It would be setting about the same time as when the sun became visible. Low-lying fog on the bank muted the landscape.

Looking out to the west, they could see the curvature of the earth at the horizon line. The sound of the 454's and the feel of the boat gliding across the surface—so smooth that it could have been hovering over the water—with the sun coming up and the moon setting, the air still cool and damp with the unsettled fog and the movement of the boat blowing a fresh-smelling breeze in their faces, the lake to themselves, still a little tired, they didn't speak: each was transfixed by the experience.

Soon they were passing the Grand Haven lighthouses, then Hoffmaster State Park and its seven miles of pristine coastline. Next was Muskegon, an industrial area, then more pristine shoreline. They followed this shoreline, out about a mile, since the water was smoother than out farther into the lake. Also, it was more interesting to have things to look at. After they passed Northport at the tip of the Leelanau Peninsula, there was no more shoreline to follow—they were out in the great lake. They passed the Manitou Islands, then headed straight toward Beaver Island.

"Hey Joe," Ramsey called. "Help me with these maps. Here, Cassandra, you steer for a bit."

"Aye, aye, captain," she said.

Joe and Ramsey looked over the section of the map with Beaver Island and its surrounding islands. "Beaver Island has the two lighthouses," Joe reminded Ramsey, "because of all the ships that ran aground over there through the years. See these charts…let's see…water is twenty feet or more up to this point, then we have to start being careful."

"Port's here," said Ramsey, "on the northeast side of Beaver," pointing at the harbor at St. James' Bay. There was a hook of land that defined the bay, terminating at Whiskey Point. "I think that's the only place to port."

"The only problem, though," said Joe, "is that it's right in town. Don't we want to go to the beach more, or maybe we should go to one of these small remote islands—say North Fox—look how small it is—we could have it all to ourselves!"

"There's no port. There's nothing there!"

"That's the point," said Joe. "We could run around there like savages."

"How would we dock? It's all rocky there, I think," said Ramsey.

"Anchor out, swim in. Or, take your raft. I don't know, we could figure it out," said Joe. "See how it looks. It would be more fun to be on a remote beach. We could motor around and look for the fish around those little islands, too. I'll help with the nav maps."

"Ask your girl, and Paul and Gina. See what they think," said Ramsey. "What do you say, Cassandra?"

"Sounds cool. We have food, beer, pot. What else would we need?" said Cassandra.

"They said it sounds great," said Joe. "They're all in."

"Okay then," said Ramsey. "You have to help me navigate in. I've never been there. Once we're close, the girls can get up on the bow and watch out for rocks. We'll need lookouts. We'll go slow. Let's see the maps. The west side of the island probably has deeper waters. The east side is between it and mainland. That's where the shipwrecks are. My dad would kill me. Wouldn't even have to go home!"

"Nothin's going to happen," said Joe. "Nothin."

"Emily and Lisa said the water's clear, so at least we can see everything," said Ramsey.

"Why don't we chill for a minute," said Cassandra. "See how clear the water is. Check out the maps. Burn one."

Ramsey immediately put in neutral and the boat glided to a stop. "Want to chill for a minute?" he called back to his passengers. "Cassandra says we should burn one."

"Is is noon yet?" asked Betty.

"Noon somewhere," replied Joe.

"Does it matter?" asked Gina. "We're on vacay!"

"It don't matter. It's just fun to ask," said Betty.

"Better break out the beer. Who's got the weed?" asked Ramsey.

"Let Paul roll one—he's got the touch," said Gina. "That's why I go out with him."

"Cause he can roll a joint?" laughed Betty. "That's all he's good for?"

"Almost. That and one other thing," said Gina.

"What other thing? Oh, he can open your beer so you don't break a nail, that's it, isn't it," said Joe.

"Yeah, that too," said Gina.

"Who wants a cold one?" asked Cassandra, rhetorically, as she handed out the beer.

"Cans. Why do we have to have cans?" said Joe. "I think the aluminum is bad for you. Bad for your brain."

"Maybe that's what happened to Paul," said Gina. "Drank too much aluminum with his beer."

"Or too much beer with his aluminum," said Joe.

"Will you guys quit rippin' on me," said Paul. "I'm pretty smart."

"Compared to what?" asked Ramsey. "Your gym rats?"

"Dumbbells," said Cassandra. "That's the other word for them. Ha."

"You guys are just jealous of my musk-kells," said Paul. "Just jealous."

"Why don't you put your musk-kells into finishing rolling that joint. I'm about ready," said Joe.

"Should be safe out here," said Ramsey, the future cop, looking around.

"Ya think?" said Cassandra. "Do ya think?"

After smoking the joint, they decided to just float around for a while. The three girls took off their outerwear, stripping down to their bikinis, then went up on the bow and spread out their towels. They laid face down on their towels and undid their tops.

"We are some lucky guys," said Ramsey. "Lucky guys!"

After a half hour, they decided to start the engines and finish the trip over to the island. The girls stayed on the bow as the boat slowly motored over in the direction of the North Fox Island. When they were within a mile of the island, Ramsey called out over the windshield. "Better put your tops on gals and be lookouts."

"Why did you have to put it that way?" said Joe.

"What was I thinking!?" said Ramsey. "What was I thinking?"

They looked at the map and decided to approach the northern tip of North Fox Island. It was shallow there, but there were no outcroppings in the area. Ramsey tilted the props half way up and watched his depth gauge. When he got in four feet of water, he raised his props more and cut the engines down to almost idle. "Small rocks ahead," said Cassandra. "The size of volleyballs is all. This might be about as far as we go. We can walk in from here. It's three, four feet deep."

"'Volleyballs,' she says," said Joe. "Anybody else would say basketballs!"

Ramsey cut the engines. "Can you throw out the anchor?" asked Ramsey.

"I'll get it," said Paul.

"Watch the boat," said Ramsey.

"I know, I know," said Paul.

"Just don't hit the boat."

Paul gave Ramsey a look. "Anchors away!" he said as he threw out the anchor, then let out forty feet of line. The wind was blowing in from the north, so the boat swung around facing the wind and floated closer to shore. They gathered up their belongings while Ramsey lowered the ladder off the stern of the boat. They blew up a small raft and placed the bulk of their stuff on it. They had a cooler with two cases of beer, some towels, sandals, a tent, and another small cooler with some food in it. The water was waist deep as they waded in to shore.

The beach was absolutely beautiful. A large dune rose up from the beach; the sand was pure white. There were pines and hardwoods growing out of the dunes, helping to stabilize the sand.

"Let's take a backpack and fill it with beer and walk around the entire island," said Joe.

"What is it—like a couple of miles?" asked Betty.

"Yeah, about a mile long and a half-mile wide, so the walk would be probably three miles," answered Joe.

"How many beers would that be?" questioned Paul.

"Well, let's see," said Joe. "Better take a 12 pack in the backpack and we can each carry one. That should do it, probably. Three beer trip, anyways, I'd say."

"A beer a mile," said Paul.

"Wow—you're getting better at math," said Gina. "That was the correct answer, wasn't it?"

"This is like a story problem in high school math," said Betty. "If there's six people and they all want to walk three miles, and they drink one beer per mile, how many beers will they drink!"

"That's 18," said Gina. "Even I know that. It's easier to figure out when there's beer involved."

"Maybe they should have had more beer in the story problems. You would of done better in math," said Paul.

They got their beer together and put on sunscreen. Paul rolled a few joints for the trip.

"You guys wearin' shoes or going barefoot?" asked Ramsey. "I'm thinkin' of going barefoot."

"I'm goin' barefoot," said Cassandra. "I want to walk in the water."

"Watch out for those man-eating fish!" said Ramsey.

"Yeah. I'm not scared. I think Lisa and Emily are out of their minds. They're cool, but they were just trying to scare us."

Everybody decided to go barefoot. "Which way?" asked Joe.

"I think we should go the shortest way," said Gina.

"What?" they all said.

"I'm kidding," said Gina. "I'm not that stupid."

THE CIGARETTE HULL BOAT TRIP

They all laughed and started out on their explorations.

The only thing they found was an abandoned airstrip cutting across the width of the island. Apparently, at one time, there had been inhabitants on the island. It was now owned by the State of Michigan. Other than that, there were no signs of human activity at all. The entire island was pristine. Some of the dunes rose a hundred plus feet from the water's edge. The water was as clear as a swimming pool. The lake was calm. Small waves lapped upon the beach. Gulls stood on the beach, flying up into the air as the group approached. The gulls seemed very unwary, perhaps even confused with their visitors. Out on the water, South Fox Island sat about four miles away. They had a good view of it as they walked down the western side of North Fox Island. As they rounded the tip, they could again see Beaver Island to the northeast. Beaver was about twelve miles away.

Returning back to where the boat was moored, they decided to pitch camp for the night. Leveling out a spot on the beach, Ramsey and Joe pitched the tent while Paul made a fire. The girls went around and collected driftwood for the fire. Ramsey went back to the boat and gathered the rest of the things they would need for the evening: a cast iron pan, silverware and plates, the sleeping bags, more beer, and two bottles of rum.

"Let's be like pirates out here and drink a bunch of rum," said Ramsey.

"Man, this is nice. No one around, just us. This is great," said Paul.

"Yeah baby," said Gina. "Gilligan's Island!"

"Wasn't there a Gina on Gilligan's Island?" asked Paul.

"I think so—the movie star?"

"No. That was Ginger!" said Cassandra.

"Oh yeah. And Mary Ann."

"Right. We got it now!"

"Maybe I should do my nails," said Gina. "Wasn't Ginger always doing her nails?"

"How about 'Castaway'? We could end up talking to volleyballs!" said Joe.

"Wilson!!!!" they all screamed.

"Cassandra talks to volleyballs all the time, don't you dear?" asked Ramsey.

"Well, yeah. Of course I do. Especially when I'm serving. 'Now, go over the net, past the redhead, and hit just inside the corner.'"

"Does it listen?" asked Paul.

"Listens better than you guys most of the time!"

"What'd she say?" kidded Ramsey.

Later that evening, they watched the sunset, drank the rum, had a huge fire, and partied. They went to bed around 2 A.M. The wind picked up a bit in the middle of the night, but settled back down around 5 A.M.

The next morning, Joe got up first. When he opened the tent flap, he saw that something was wrong.

"Ramsey! Ramsey!! Ramsey!!!"

"What?"

"Get out here!"

"What's so important?"

"Your boat is way out there!"

"What !!??" Ramsey hurried out of the tent in his undies. The boat was at least a half mile out.

Joe got up when he heard about the boat. "Dude, the anchor didn't grip right."

"Okay. We've got to think," said Ramsey. "What direction is the wind blowing?"

"Toward us," said Paul, "Which is good!"

"Well, I can walk half way out there," said Ramsey, "then swim the rest of the way. I left the key in there. What else do I need? Anything?"

"You're a good swimmer, go for it," said Paul.

"Bring it in and I'll make sure the anchor catches this time. This could have been bad!" said Joe. "I thought it seemed secure when we anchored it. I'm sorry. This shouldn't have happened."

"At least it didn't float away!" said Ramsey. "I'd have some explaining to do to Papa!"

"You okay?" asked Paul of Ramsey.

"Yeah. See you in a minute."

Ramsey walked out until he was up to his chest, then started swimming out to the boat. Paul and Joe could hardly see him after a few minutes. They could see some splashing and were confident in his swimming abilities. After ten minutes, they heard the engines fire.

"Alright!!!" yelled Paul. He high-fived Joe.

They watched as the boat approached, then went out in the water to help Ramsey.

"Man," yelled Ramsey. "The depth gauge said the water was forty feet out there—about the same as the anchor rope. One more breeze and the anchor would have fallen off the ledge. We got lucky!!!"

"We're livin' right," said Paul. Ramsey threw the anchor over toward Paul. "Let's take it in closer to shore this time and I'll get the anchor on a rock. There's some rocks that are pretty big. I'll tie the puppy onto it. We're not losing it again!"

Ramsey cut the engines. Paul and Joe pulled the boat toward shore. In an instant, Joe was pulled beneath the water. A plume of blood stained the water. Paul's eyes widened as he realized what was happening, then he started running through the water toward shore. Ramsey dove into the water to try to save Joe, even though he knew it probably was too late. His police training made him react spontaneously. He could not find Joe and watched Paul as he ran frantically through the water. Then, suddenly, Paul looked as though he had been tackled. He fell into the water, thrashed around a bit, screamed once, then everything went silent. Ramsey saw a fin surface between him and the boat. He decided to make a run for it to the beach, but he was cut down within a few feet. All three guys were dead.

After a half hour, the three girls got out of the tent.

"Where's the guys?"

"Something about the boat. They woke me up a bit ago when they were yelling about something."

"The boat's right there. It's okay."

"They're probably doing a 'wake and bake' out there, smoking a joint without us."

"They'll be in in a minute. Want to make a fire—there's still coals. I'll throw on some wood," said Cassandra. She got the fire going and they sat around watching it.

Cassandra yelled out to the boat: "Hey you morons!!! Get in here!"

"You guys better not be smokin' all the dope," yelled Betty. Then she looked at Gina. "I'm getting hungry."

"Maybe they're not out there," said Betty. "Maybe they took a walk or something."

"Well, I'm going to work on my tan," said Cassandra. "That fire warmed me up just fine."

Cassandra took off the jogging outfit she had worn to bed. She still had her bikini on underneath.

"You know," she said. "No one's around. I'm getting rid of my bikini line," she said as she took off her top.

She got the sleeping bag and pillow out of the tent and laid it on the beach. "This is the life," she said.

"Good plan," said Gina. "I'm following suit." She went into the tent and got her bag and pillow, as well as Betty's. "Care to join us," she said as she removed her top.

Betty laid down on the sleeping bag and took off her top, too.

"Who needs those guys," stated Gina.

After a while, Cassandra decided to walk down the beach. Her purpose was two-fold: she was getting restless and felt like she needed to exercise and she wanted to see if she could find the guys. She snapped her bikini top around her waist just so she'd have it with her and started walking on the wet sand. After walking for a half mile, she decided to walk naked, so removed her suit completely and held it in her hand. It felt great walking naked. Stretching her arms as she walked, Cassandra felt very free.

Deciding to go for a quick dip, she tossed her bikini onto the sand and waded out into the shallow water. She got out to her waist and dove in, getting her head completely wet. Splashing water onto her face, Cassandra rubbed her eyes and cleansed herself. The water felt fresh and invigorating. She dove in again, then stood up and shook the water from her hair. Walking back to the sand, she decided to sit down by a piece of driftwood and just think about things.

Yoga was a passing interest of hers, so she assumed the lotus position, closing her eyes and purging her mind of stray thoughts. The morning sun felt wonderful on her naked body. The sound of waves lapping upon the beach was the only sound she could hear. 'I'm not going to think about anything,' she thought, 'not even thinking about not thinking.' With her eyes closed and with the sound of the waves, she began to reach a state of bliss.

Out in the water, several hundred feet from shore, a fin began to surface. The fish swam parallel to shore, going north, then switched directions, beginning to swim south. It swam a hundred or more feet in each direction, changing directions again and again. Each time it changed directions, it came a little closer to shore. It was swimming out from shore directly in front of Cassandra.

Maintaining her lotus position, Cassandra began to chant "ommmmmmm, ommmmmmmm, ommmmmmm."

The fish began to get closer to shore. Once it reached water only two foot deep, the fish stopped swimming parallel to shore. It was out fifty feet from the beach. It turned toward the beach and slowly began to direct itself toward Cassandra. At twenty-four feet long, the fish weighed over four hundred pounds. When it reached water that was less than eighteen inches deep, it began crawling on its pectoral fins, pushing itself along with its tail. Slowly and silently, it kept approaching Cassandra. When it reached water only six inches deep, most of its body was out of the water, but it kept moving, pushing itself along, not swimming, crawling. It was six feet from Cassandra, right at the edge of the water, when it raised itself on its pectoral fins so that virtually all of its body was out of the water, then it stood up on its tail, arched its body and swiped over Cassandra, cleanly removing her head. The rest of her body remained untouched and didn't move, still in the lotus position. The fish splashed back into the water and swam away with her head. For a few seconds, Cassandra continued to think.

Her heart continued to beat for those few seconds, squirting blood out from her ravaged neck, the blood flowing down her body like chocolate down a chocolate fountain. Cassandra had a chocolate fountain at her high school graduation party. Then, when her heart stopped beating, the chocolate just oozed from her neck, running down her body, staining the sand she was sitting upon.

Back at the campsite, Gina was starting to get restless and Betty was starting to get hungry again. Gina threw another log on the fire and stirred it while Betty made two sandwiches.

"I wonder where everybody is," said Betty.

"And Cassandra. What. Did she decide to walk around the whole island again?"

"She went around that way," said Betty, pointing down the beach. "Maybe we should walk around the other way and intercept her. She would have been back by now if she wasn't walking around the island."

"She's a health freak," said Gina.

"Well, I could use a little exercise," said Betty, tugging at a little extra flesh around her waist.

"Maybe they're all on the other side of the island. Might as well go looking for them, what else can we do?"

They finished their sandwiches and started walking topless down the beach. They each held their top in one of their hands.

Betty stopped repeatedly to pick up small stones and shells. They walked slowly, enjoying the morning but concerned with the whereabouts of the rest of their party. Betty used her top to hold her collection of stones and shells.

"Where are those guys," Betty kept saying.

There was a low area on the beach where water collected in a large pool. Large pieces of driftwood littered the area, some of it in the pool of water and some of it around the edges. They walked through the pool of water. It was twenty degrees warmer than the lake. They stood in the warm water.

"What if the whole lake was this warm," said Betty. "That would feel really good!"

"Just like bathwater," responded Gina.

Behind them, hidden aside a log lying in the water, a carp was sticking his head out from his burrow. He slowly emerged while Gina and Betty talked about the warm pool of water. The carp silently exited the burrow and then suddenly leapt into the air and snatched Betty around the waist, sailing through the air toward the water. In an instant, she was gone. The carp took her into the water and swam away with Betty's body hanging out from its mouth. Gina stood paralyzed for a moment, dropped her bikini top, screamed and ran back down the beach toward the campsite. She kept looking behind her as she ran, running fast, running as fast as she had ever run.

She reached the campsite, and looked frantically around her. She surveyed her surroundings. She looked in the water and on land for carp. Everything was quiet. There were no carp in sight. The boat was moored out in the water about 150 feet out from shore. There was the campfire burning, the tent, and the sleeping bags spread on the ground. A few bottles of rum, empty, rested against a log they had used as a bench the night before.

She thought about running to the top of the dune behind her—but where would she go from there? Would the carp be able to find her on top of the dune? Probably not, she thought, but was this a good place to stick around—no! 'I need to get out of here,' she thought. 'But how?'

Gina quickly looked all around her, again. 'The boat. How can I get to the boat? I need to get to the boat. Am I alone here? I think I am. Otherwise, someone would be here by now. I am alone here. Somehow, everybody else is gone. I need to get to the boat. Can I drive the boat? I can try. I watched Ramsey a little bit.'

She looked at the water. There was no activity. She looked at the boat. 'I could get there in one minute, I think,' she thought. 'Run? Go silently? A little of both? Go silently first. Be quiet. Then run like hell to the boat. I need to get to the boat.'

Looking again around her, Gina first saw the raft, but there were no paddles—they had pulled it into shore. She then looked at the tent. She thought about the tent poles. Going inside the tent, she knocked it down and took two poles—the ones with sharp points that stick into the ground—grabbing them like a native in the jungle would grab a spear. She was unaware that she still had no top on. That was the least of her concerns. She held a pole in each hand, and slowly started out into the water.

There still was no activity in the water, she made sure of that. Gradually wading out, looking behind her too, she made her way toward the boat. Walking faster now, she was within sixty feet of it. The ladder was still down, off from the stern of the boat. Looking back behind her again, Gina determined that the quicker she made it to the boat, the better. She was waist deep in the water. Everything was quiet, so she slowly submerged her body in the water. Holding both poles in one hand, she silently swam to the ladder doing a side stroke. Grabbing the ladder, she put her foot on the bottom step. Throwing the poles up into the boat, she hoisted herself onto the boat.

Gina went to the bow and pulled at the anchor line. The boat started moving toward the anchor as she reeled in the forty foot of rope. Constantly looking around her, she pulled in all the rope, and hoisted the anchor into the boat. She went to the back and pulled up the ladder.

Going over to the console, she looked at the dashboard and saw the key in the ignition. She turned the key and the engines fired. Remembering watching Ramsey, she pushed in the release button for the throttle and pushed forward on it. The boat began moving. Steering it out away from the island, Gina slowly moved away from the shore. The props were all the way up; water was thrown forty feet behind the boat. She looked over the controls and found the tilt, pushing the button to lower the props. They quit throwing water as she moved away from the island. 'Where to?' she thought. 'Where am I headed?'

Beaver Island was directly in front of her, over twelve miles away. 'I am going there,' she thought.

Gina aimed for the island, almost straight north. Gaining confidence, she throttled the boat higher and reached 50 MPH. She stood behind the wheel so that she had a good view of the waters ahead, the wind blowing her hair back, her left hand on top of the windshield to balance herself, her right hand on the wheel. She thought about the guys talking about the island and the port on the north end of the island. Banking the boat hard, she remembered hearing that the waters were deeper on the west side of the island, so she steered in that direction. She would go past the west side of the island, then around the northern tip to the port. The last thing she wanted to do was to hit an outcropping. The day had been rough enough already.

A minute after she went around the southern tip of the island, she saw another boat about a half mile out from shore. She headed toward that boat. The boat was just sitting out in the water, apparently drifting. She could see two men inside the boat. She kept heading toward it. As she approached, she throttled down and waved. They waved back.

"I'm in trouble," she yelled over the engines. She turned the ignition off. "Help me!"

The two men looked at each other. Gina: young, gorgeous, and topless was waving frantically at them. "Stay there," one yelled. "We'll come to you."

They started their engine and motored over to her. "What's up?"

"I need to get to Beaver Island. I don't know how to drive!"

"Who is with you?"

"Nobody."

"Why do you need to go to the island?"

"I've lost my friends. Help me!"

The two men looked at each other. "Why don't you take her in, Chad, you used to have one of those boats."

Chad got into the boat and looked at Gina. "Do you know you don't have a shirt on," he asked. She looked down at herself and covered her breasts with her arms. Finding a man's white button-down shirt, she put it on. "I need to find the police. I know there's a cop on the island. McFadden, right?"

"Yep. What do you mean you lost your friends?"

"One got eaten by a carp. I saw it myself."

"That's the third one I've heard of. Didn't believe it at first. Really—you saw this?"

"I was right beside her. She got eaten by a carp!"

"What is this world coming to? I'll meet you back on the island," Chad said to his partner. Chad started the engines and started heading to the port. He throttled the boat and reached St. James Harbor in minutes. Throttling down, he entered the harbor and motored over to where his slip was. He moored the boat and helped Gina get onto the dock.

"My truck is over here. Come on."

Chad pointed out his vehicle to Gina. "It's a '48 Chevy pickup," he said. "Completely restored."

"I like the color," said Gina. It was bright sky blue. "How far is it to the cop shop?"

"We'll be there before the engine even warms up," said Chad.

He opened the passenger door for Gina, then shut it carefully. "Don't slam the door," he advised Gina, as he ran around to the other side, got in and turned the truck on. The keys had been left in the ignition. Backing up, Chad headed to the police station.

McFadden was sitting on the front porch watching people walk by. Chad pulled up to let Gina do the explaining. She got out of the truck and left the door partially open so she didn't close it wrong and ran up to McFadden. "My friends...I think they all maybe got eaten by carp! Help me, help me!"

After Gina explained what happened, McFadden took her inside the station. "Thanks, Chad. I'll take it from here."

CHAPTER FOURTEEN
THE RECOVERY MISSION

Officer McFadden got on the phone immediately. First he called the coast guard and ordered a boat to go to the island and search it for survivors. He also ordered a plane to pick up Lisa and Emily. "Get Lisa and Emily over to North Fox Island ASAP. We'll meet you on the airstrip. I'll take the chopper over there."

"I know them," said Gina. "Lisa and Emily."

"What?"

"I met them in Grand Haven. That's why we're here. They told us not to come."

"They told you not to come and that's why you're here?" asked McFadden.

"We didn't believe them. The guys I was with thought it was bull. They wanted to prove them wrong."

"We've had two fish attacks. It's no bull."

"We didn't believe it. I believe it now—I saw it with my own eyes. She got taken away by a bigass carp."

"How about everybody else?" asked McFadden.

"I don't know, but they weren't around. We couldn't find anybody."

"How many?"

"Five missing. Three guys, two girls. Well, one girl is missing, the other one got eaten by a carp. I know that much."

"Where were the guys?"

"Gone. Gone when we woke up. There was something about the boat. It drifted out or something. They brought it in. It looked okay when we got up. We thought they were on it messing around. It was even in closer to shore than where we left it. I don't know what happened. Then Cassandra took a walk and never came back and we went looking for her, Betty and me, and then she got eaten by the carp. It is a carp, right? It was so big and it was flying through the air."

"What?" said McFadden.

"You know, flying, leaping, whatever, it was going through the air and grabbed Betty right in the center of her body and sailed into the water and took her away."

"So, how big was this carp?"

"From here to there," said Gina, pointing from wall to wall in the office. "It wouldn't fit on that wall right there if it was mounted."

"That's twenty-four feet," said McFadden. Just then the phone rang. It was Lisa.

"What's going on?" she questioned.

"Carp attack. North Fox Island. Might be as many as five people. We don't know. Just a sec."

He turned to Gina. "What's your name, honey?"

"Gina."

"Someone here knows you. Gina."

"What's she got to do with it?"

"She was there. She's okay."

"Who's not okay?"

"Maybe everybody else, we don't know."

"What!? Put her on."

"Gina!" said Lisa. "What's happening?"

"Those guys wanted to go to Beaver Island but then decided to go to North Fox and we spent the night and everybody disappeared except for Betty and we were walking down the beach looking for them and this giant carp jumped out of the sand and ate Betty and took her into the lake and I don't know where everybody else is maybe they're okay, I hope so but I don't know and I came to Beaver and found McFadden and he called you and I know you told us not to go but they weren't afraid and now I don't know where everybody else is and maybe they're okay but I don't know."

"Okay, okay. Wait a minute. Calm down here," said Lisa. "Did you say the carp jumped out of the sand?"

"He was in one of those shallow ponds just a bit away from the edge of the water. We called them 'tidal pools' in Florida. He was there, behind a log, I think, in the water, but it was shallow. He was down in a hole behind the log, I think, it happened so fast, he jumped out, we didn't see him when we went past, but he had to be there and the water was ankle deep, so he must have been in a hole and he jumped out and Betty…she just was in his mouth and he went into the lake and she was gone."

"Okay, okay," said Lisa. "Emily and I are coming right now. We'll go to the island and see what we can find out. Tell McFadden where this happened so we know where to start looking."

"I want to go there, too," said Gina. "I'll show you. I want to find them."

"Ask McFadden. See what he says. It's up to him. It might be better for you to stay there. Either way, I'll be in touch," said Lisa.

McFadden hung up the phone. "You should stay here. Draw a diagram of where you last saw everybody."

"No." said Gina. "I need to go. I can help."

"Alright, I guess. It would be helpful if we knew where this flying carp was hanging out."

"Thanks. I sure hope we find the guys and Cassandra."

"Okay," said McFadden. "Let's keep our hopes up. Come on, get in the squad car and we'll go to the chopper. You got another shirt?"

"No."

"Ah....whatever. Come on," said McFadden.

He began driving over to the airport while calling the coroner. "We may have something for you. Don't know yet. Another carp attack. I'll let you know. Giving fair warning. Could be five. I'll be in touch."

They went to the helipad on the edge of the airport and choppered over to North Fox Island. It would be an hour or more before Lisa and Emily arrived. The coast guard boat was motoring around the island, moving slowly, looking for either a survivor or a body. McFadden flew the chopper low over the water, peering down through the glass floor looking for anything out of the ordinary. He was looking for a survivor, a big fish, and body parts. He thought about likelihoods: 1) a big fish, 2) body parts, and 3) a survivor. Gina pointed out the tent, which was unnecessary, since it was plain as day. The fire was still smoking, too. She also pointed out the log by the tidal pool where Betty was attacked. "That was helpful," McFadden said. "At least we know where that is."

He radioed the coast guard boat. "Anything?"

"Negative."

"Roger that," responded McFadden.

"Hold tight," they added. "Maybe we do have something."

A coast guard recruit was on the bridge of the boat with his binoculars. He was scouring the water and also the beach. He re-focused his binoculars and directed them toward Cassandra. Laying down the binoculars, he rubbed his eyes and re-focused again. She still was in the lotus position, in perfect form, just missing her head.

The recruit called over an officer. "Tell me I'm crazy," he said.

The officer took one look, then radioed back. "We have found one deceased."

"Location?" asked McFadden.

"Beach. West side. Toward the south. Female. That's all I can say."

"Will you go recover?" asked McFadden.

"On our way."

The chopper flew over to the area mentioned. McFadden got out his binoculars and took a quick look.

"On second thought, you'd better wait until the biologists come. Do not disturb the deceased."

"Roger that."

The chopper circled the island several times while waiting for Lisa and Emily. The coast guard had an inflatable boat that they off-loaded with two men and a body bag. The inflatable made it to shore.

McFadden spotted the plane approaching and moved the chopper away from the landing strip. The plane buzzed over the island once, checking out the condition of the strip—it hadn't been used for years and the pilot had never landed there. He then banked the plane hard, the wings almost vertical, came around again, and landed perfectly on the strip.

McFadden flew the chopper over to where the plane had landed, spotting the chopper off to the side of the strip. Emily and Lisa got out of the plane. Jack, the pilot, got out as well. Gina ran over to Lisa and Emily and gave them hugs. "We only found one. It must be Cassandra. They said she is dead! We looked for the guys and we can't find them," Gina said. "We never should have come!"

"Let's keep our hopes up," said Emily.

"This is Jack, Captain Jack, Captain Jack Summers," said Lisa. "He said he'd help us look around."

"How should we do this, officer?" said Emily.

McFadden went to the chopper and got two shotguns. "Here, Jack. I suppose they showed you how to use one of these in the guard, huh?"

"Oh yeah," he responded. "Used to shoot trap and skeet a lot, too. May need to nail a flying fish, I heard."

"I don't know what's going on. It's crazy. First a hermit got eaten up in the water, then a young girl got her legs chomped off, now flying fish, I don't know what to tell ya. People were scared enough before, and now this. Where will it end?" said McFadden.

Working their way down the dune toward Cassandra, McFadden warned the girls about what they might witness. He remembered their reaction to the hermit. "It ain't going to be pretty," he said.

After walking down the dune, they turned and walked south down the beach. Cassandra was a half mile down. The coast guard was there waiting for them. "Wait here," the cop said to the girls. "Let me see about this first." McFadden and Captain Jack walked toward the crime scene. It seemed unbelievable. McFadden didn't know what to say, so he made a joke. "Anything unusual, gentlemen?"

Looking at him and not knowing what to say created a long silence. Finally, one of the coast guard personnel spoke. "It's the craziest thing I've ever seen."

"Roger that," said McFadden. "Roger that."

"We photographed her already. There's just her bikini and her footprints, nothing else but this slash in the sand. Now what?"

"Maybe the biologists should give her a look. I don't know. I'll ask them." He went over to Lisa and Emily. "Ah, okay, so I don't know if you need to see this, but she is missing her head and that's all."

"That's all?" stated Emily. "That's all!?"

"What I'm trying to say is that there's no other damage to her body. Do you think you want to see how she was recovered before she is removed?"

"Honestly, I'm getting a little tired of looking at bodies," said Lisa.

"There're some marks in the sand. That might be important. The marks could have been made by one of your fish."

"They're not our fish," said Lisa.

"Maybe we should take a look," said Emily. "Stay here, Gina."

They both approached the body. Cassandra looked so peaceful, it didn't bother Emily or Lisa the way they thought it might. Or, maybe they were just getting hardened.

They saw Cassandra's footsteps embedded in the sand showing where she had walked down the beach, then leading to the edge of the water and then up to the place where she had sat down on the beach. Her bikini was tossed over to the one side. On the other side of her were spots of dislodged sand leading from the water. These areas were about four feet apart. There was also the large swipe in the sand right at the water's edge. Gauging the distance between the smaller marks in the sand, the girth of the fish would be about three feet.

"Photograph everything in the sand," Lisa said to the coast guard. "Then, you can move her. We'll talk to the coroner about seeing if there's any teeth left in her neck. She doesn't deserve to be prodded right now. Let's give her some respect."

"Wow," said Emily. "You're getting good at this."

"Maybe I'm building a wall or something. I really liked her."

"I know. Me too," said Emily. "She was a beautiful girl."

"Our work's not done," said McFadden. "We need to check out the tent and find the area where Betty was attacked."

They decided to go toward the collapsed tent first, then to the location where Betty had met her demise. McFadden and Captain Jack checked out their guns and loaded them. McFadden and the Captain walked side by side, each holding their gun to the outside. Lisa and Emily walked with Gina between them. Gina was the most nervous of the group, constantly looking behind her. She often walked backward on the beach, searching behind her for danger.

Reaching the camping area, the Captain and McFadden looked inside the tent. There were still three sleeping bags inside but that was all. The other bags were still spread out on the ground.

"We took the bags out and caught some rays while we were waiting for the guys to return," explained Gina. "I tore the tent down to get the poles."

"You were going to spear a fish?" asked McFadden.

"I don't know. Yes, I would have. It was all I could think of. I'm glad I didn't have to use them."

Walking farther down the beach, they spoke of the beauty of the area. Beaver Island looked amazing in the distance. The white sand of North Fox Island was a lovely sight. Gentle waves lapped upon the beach. The sky was clear and bright blue. The only sounds were from the gulls, still startled by having visitors. The pines on the island provided a wonderful scent. It seemingly could not have been more perfect.

Getting close to the area where Betty was attacked, Gina provided a forewarning. Stopping, she pointed ahead the 100 feet to the log lying in the pool of water. "There. It's right there where it happened. See the log. The thing was under it or beside it or in a hole by it but we walked right by and didn't see it and then it came right out suddenly and just grabbed Betty!"

They began walking slowly, focusing on whether or not they could see an area the fish could live in.

"Why would it be on the beach?" the captain asked.

"They are starting to grow suprabranchial organs," said Emily.

"English?" insisted the captain.

"They are, simply put, extensions of the gills of a fish so it can breathe out of water," said Lisa.

"Mudpuppies have them," said Emily.

"Other things, too," said Lisa. "We found these carp developing them a while back but never found any on land. They are evolving quickly."

Approaching the area, McFadden asked the girls to stay where they were. Nobody argued. The captain and McFadden approached cautiously. They both had their guns aimed at the area. Gina looked around nervously. It looked the same as any puddle on the beach.

"Let me come and look," said Emily.

"Okay. Nothing's here," said the cop.

Emily went over there while Lisa stayed with Gina.

She took a stick and started probing in the puddle by the log. The ground was firm everywhere she poked, but then she found an area where her stick easily penetrated the sand. She poked around a little more. "Lisa, come here."

Lisa went to the area. "See here. Look. This looks like it could be an area where the fish hides down in the mud—remember the mudpuppy video."

Gina stood back twenty feet. "Gina. Come here."

"Is this the area you think it came from?" asked Emily.

"It came from behind, so I can't say for sure, but yes, somewhere right in there."

"If that's true," said Lisa, "then these have made the evolutionary leap from water to land."

"So," added Emily, "they would still need water to live but could live out of water for a while. There's lots of species like that."

"You're saying that now these things are going to be attacking people on land?" McFadden questioned.

"It attacked Betty on land," said Gina. "I saw that with my own eyes."

"Could it still be down there?" asked the captain.

"Could be anywhere," said Lisa. "Once something makes a burrow, they stay with it for a while usually, so I'd guess that if it isn't there now, it will be back sometime. I can't guess when."

McFadden took the stick and probed deeper in the hole. "I don't feel anything. I don't think it's there now."

"It could have a tunnel from the water to this area, sort of like a muskrat. It might come and go," said Lisa.

"Let's keep walking," said the cop. "See if we can find anything."

Gina kept looking behind her as they walked away from the area. She had a bad experience there.

They walked halfway around the island, then up the dune on the backside of the landing strip. Everything seemed absolutely normal. "We'll check it out again tomorrow," said McFadden. I'll get the tent and bags then too, just in case there's anything we could possibly derive from them. It doesn't seem as though they would be important. You never know."

"I can stay on the island—Beaver Island—tonight and maybe help tomorrow. I don't know how to say this, but maybe something could wash up on the shore tomorrow," said Captain Jack.

"That would be great," said McFadden. "I talked to this gal I know that runs the local motel and set up a room for Lisa and Emily. I'll get one for you, too. You'll like the place. I guess I'll set up Gina with a room, too."

"Be just like a vacation, except for the purpose of being here," he said.

"Yeah, well, what are you going to do?" said McFadden. "I guess it's all work. If we didn't love the work, we wouldn't do it. Sometimes, though, it's a little rough."

"Yeah, today was a little rough," said the captain. "The worst part is having to tell the families—you gotta do that?"

"Mainland. I call mainland. They track 'em down. State boys usually take care of it. Do it personally. Means more to the families. Tough job. I've done it on the island. Don't like it. What are ya going to do, though. Someone has to be the bearer of bad news," said McFadden.

"Yeah, college kids, too. Let's see what we can find tomorrow," said the captain. "Well, it's back to Beaver Island."

After making it back to the island, they set their plans in motion for the evening.

"You guys get checked in and cleaned up and we'll go over to the nice restaurant tonight and spend some of my expense account. Gotta burn through a little cash one way or another. This seems like as good of a time as any," said McFadden.

They went over to the motel and got checked in, showered, and got ready to go over to the local restaurant. Gina had nothing to wear except for what she had on—which wasn't much—so she decided to look around town and buy some clothes and a new bikini top to wear the next day. The captain spotted her $100. Lisa, Emily, and the captain walked over to the local restaurant. There were white linens on the tables. The silverware was heavy and was wrapped in stiff white linen napkins. McFadden had already arrived and had taken a table off to the side—out of hearing range—just in case business came up. Emily and Lisa were hoping that business would not come up this evening; they were hoping to forget the day's events for a little while. McFadden was out of uniform and had already ordered a pitcher. Lisa noticed that it was half gone already.

"Got a head start on us, huh McFadden?" said Emily. "Rough day at the beach?"

"Yeah, rough day at the beach."

"Can we talk about something else," said Lisa. "I'd like to talk about something pleasant, or anything else, really. Even war or something."

"Ah, yeah. The good old days in 'Nam," the captain said. "The stories I could tell."

"How many tours?" asked McFadden.

"Here we go," said Emily. "You had to say that, Lisa?"

"Oh, sorry gals, two tours. That's all I'll say. Two long grueling tours, walking through the jungle, hunting down the enemy. Except we never knew who the enemy was—unless they were shooting at us, then we knew. But most of the people there were just regular people. Never knew who to trust. You never know."

"Well, you can trust us," said Lisa, trying to change the topic. "Can't he, Emily?"

"Oh yeah. Any kids, captain?"

The captain brightened. "Yep, got two in college. That's why it was painful today," he said, lowering his voice again.

"Wonderful," said Emily, trying to get the conversation to cheer up. "What are they going in to?"

"Well, the boy doesn't know what he wants to go into yet but my girl is studying mortuary science."

Emily and Lisa looked at each other.

"Oh, that's an interesting field," said McFadden. "The coroner we deal with is really good, isn't he?" he said to Emily.

"Oh yeah. Very helpful," she replied a bit flatly. "Say, captain, where'd you learn to fly a plane like that—the landing was impressive!"

"Nam. Did two tours there. Two long grueling tours."

Later, they decided to get an early start the next day so that they could cover every square inch of North Fox Island. It was decided that Gina would be able to come along as well.

CHAPTER FIFTEEN
SEARCHING NORTH FOX ISLAND

Captain Jack, Lisa, and Emily climbed in the plane. The captain radioed the Beaver Island Airport, notifying them that he was ready to fly. Permission was granted and they lifted into the air and headed toward North Fox Island. Meanwhile, McFadden and Gina hopped into the chopper and headed in the same direction. The captain radioed McFadden as soon as he was in the clear.

"We're in the air headed toward North Fox. Thought we'd buzz the other islands for a sec to see if there's anything unusual."

"Okay with me," McFadden replied. "Burn some fuel."

"Roger that. Will catch up with you in just a few."

They flew low over the small islands in the area. Lisa and Emily kept a watch out for dark shadows in the water. They figured that there would have to be more fish somewhere in the vicinity. The sun was out bright and the shallow water was bright turquoise. It would be easy to see a large fish against the bright sandy bottom around the islands. The little islands were beautiful and very remote. Only the Manitou Islands were populated, and only with tourists. The State of Michigan Park System owned those islands. Lisa and Emily noticed that nobody was out swimming.

"They've taken our warnings—see," said Emily.

"Who wouldn't. You'd have to be stupid to swim out there with what's happened."

"Our friends weren't too bright."

"They just were boneheaded, that's all. Not everybody listens," said Lisa.

"After this news gets out tomorrow, people will listen," said Emily. "After today we'll be sure that there are no survivors. Probably have to do a news conference. Release the names tomorrow unless something miraculous happens today. I'm not expecting anything."

"Me neither, unfortunately."

"Keep your fingers crossed. That's all."

They headed over to the landing strip. Captain Jack landed the plane perfectly again. McFadden and Gina were waiting for them by the chopper.

"Find anything?" asked McFadden.

"Negative," responded Lisa.

"No one swimming at Manitou. That's good," said Emily. "People are taking our warnings, maybe."

"Hope so. Well, where to start, where to start," said McFadden.

Lisa spoke up first: "It's about a mile and a half if we go down to the water here and walk around the southern part of the island first, then we could come back up here—I packed some sandwiches and stuff for lunch—do lunch, walk around the northern part, look around the campsite, etc., see what is over there. I want to look around where Betty was taken, too. We can do that last—if that sounds okay with you officer."

"Yeah, that's fine. Six of one, half dozen of another," said McFadden. He grabbed a backpack with some supplies in it and two shotguns and gave one to the captain. "Loaded and ready, sir," said McFadden.

"I hope we see a flying fish," said Captain Jack. "Be like shootin' a big skeet, except for the splat. Those skeet don't really make much sound, but I like how they look when they shatter. You shoot skeet, boss?"

"Used to," replied McFadden. "Used to do it in the UP when I was in school. Lots of fun!"

"Oh yeah," said the captain. "How 'bout you girls…any trap or skeet shooting?"

"No," they replied. "Sounds like fun, though. Maybe we can throw you up some pieces of driftwood or something later on and keep you in practice," Emily said.

"Yeah. I'm sort of itching to pull this trigger!" said the captain. "But first, we should work."

They went down the dune to the beach and started walking the shoreline. The waves today were larger, about two and a half feet, so they came ashore more than they had the day before. This meant that there was a bit less walking distance from the water's edge to the toe of the dune. Instead of walking three abreast, Gina walked directly behind the cop and the captain. She felt safer there.

The captain fidgeted with his shotgun every now and then. He checked several times to make sure there was a shell loaded. He played with the safety, flipping it on and off. "Shell still in there, captain," Lisa teased him.

"Yeah, still there," he replied. "Just want to make sure I'm prepared."

After walking around half the island, there was no trace of anything, living or dead, other than the gulls.

"Just a bunch of dumb Laridae," said Emily.

"Yep," said Lisa.

The captain gave a puzzled look.

"Laridae—gulls. It's their fancy name," said Emily.

"Well, aren't you two high faluten! Laridae. I'll have to remember that," said the captain.

"Kind like saying 'hasenpfeffer' for rabbit," said Lisa. "Why eat rabbit when you could eat hasenpfeffer?"

"Ah yes, I see where you're going with this. Like 'vino.' 'I'll have another glass of vino.'"

"Exactly," said Emily. "Now you're a class act."

"It's not so much what it is, it's how you look at it," said the captain.

They walked up to the landing strip and grabbed lunch, then back down to continue around the island.

Approaching the campsite, McFadden took a rope and a large canvas bag out of his backpack. "We can bundle up the tent and sleeping bags, stick them in this canvas bag for now. I'll tie this rope onto the bag, then tie a loop and I can hook it on the way out of here. Will save carrying it."

"Good plan," said Lisa. "Now, is there anything we are looking for in the tent. Anything you can think of, Gina?"

"We'll just empty it out. All we did was sleep in there. We got a little wasted on rum that night. We all just crashed out."

McFadden held the collapsed tent up so that Lisa could climb inside.

Lisa looked in the tent and started tossing out the sleeping bags. That was all there was. "Nothing, just as we thought," she said. "Do you want to look in here, Inspector Cousteau," she said to McFadden.

"I'm good. No need," he replied.

They stuffed the tent, sleeping bags, and remaining poles into the canvas bag, as well as the coolers and some empty bottles of run. He tied the raft onto the large bag. McFadden tied a rope around all of it and made a large loop at the top so that he could hook it with a grappling hook dangling from the chopper. They looked around the fire area to make sure that there was nothing else around. Next, they proceeded toward the area where Betty was attacked by the carp.

Arriving there, the captain took a long stick and started poking around the area where Gina thought the fish had been hiding. The ground was firm in the entire area except for one spot behind the large log lying in the water. McFadden looked out in the water for an entrance hole, as was described by Emily and Lisa.

"You don't mind do you?" McFadden asked before taking off his pants. "I'd like to go out a bit farther and don't want to be wet all day."

"I don't know," said Lisa. "Whitey-tighties?"

"No," said McFadden, stretching out the waistband of his pants and peering down. "Today I think I have on my shark-themed boxers!"

"Topical," said Emily.

"As long as they're not Fred Flintstone undies. I might lose respect for you!" said Gina.

"Or Power Rangers," laughed Lisa.

McFadden shook his head and removed his pants. Cartoonish sharks decorated the boxers.

"Friendly-looking guys. Very nice. Did your mom buy those for you?" asked Emily.

"Probably for Christmas," McFadden answered. "Actually, a girlfriend bought them for me."

"You have a girlfriend?" questioned Emily. "Somehow I thought you were like Andy of Mayberry—he seemed pretty alone most of the time."

"It was an old girlfriend," he replied.

"How old?" kidded Emily. "Over eighty?"

Gina laughed. "I bet you have your pick of all the girls on Beaver Island. You're sort of a hottie."

"Sort of a hottie," McFadden said. "Sort of a hottie."

"Okay, you are a hottie. Feel better now?" said Gina.

"Yeah, that's better. But to answer your question, there's five hundred fifty absolutely wonderful people on the island, and that includes two hundred hermits, two hundred that are over sixty, and the other hundred fifty has a hundred guys in it, so that leaves another fifty and they're all older than me, married, gay, not interested in me, or something—there's not a lot of fish in this pond for a guy that's thirty."

He prodded the bottom with a stick. "Hey, here's something. It's like a tunnel!"

Lisa rolled up her pants. The cop was out to just above his knees. She waded out to see what he had found. "That's similar to a muskrat tunnel," she said. "And it leads to the shore by the log."

She went over by the log. The captain was prodding the hole with the stick in one hand and the shotgun in the other. He was on his hands and knees. Suddenly, the carp sprang from the hole and latched onto the captain's face.

The captain swung his shotgun around and fired once into the carp's body, just below its gills. The carp went limp and fell to the beach. The captain was missing part of his nose; it was bleeding profusely.

McFadden ripped off his own shirt and bundled it up, applying direct pressure to the captain's nose. The carp began sliding down into its burrow. "Get the carp," McFadden yelled. "Get the carp."

Gina sprung into action. She grabbed the carp by the gills to keep it from sliding down into its burrow. Lisa and Emily, recovering from the sudden shock, then grabbed the carp and helped Gina pull it from the burrow.

"Hello!!!!" yelled McFadden, still holding the captain's head. "I have never seen a fish that big."

The three girls tugged on the carp, extracting it from the hole little by little until it was totally out of its burrow. Its eyes were open, as was its mouth—displaying large incisors.

"Darn," said Gina. "Broke two nails!"

The captain's face and neck were covered with blood. McFadden's shirt was saturated.

"Let's get the captain up to the chopper," said McFadden. "We've got to get him to the doc."

They worked their way up the dune and got the captain in the chopper. Everybody piled in and McFadden handled the controls as Lisa applied pressure to the captain. "Call the doc," he ordered Emily. "Tell him what happened. We'll be there in fifteen minutes."

The doc was now on McFadden's speed dial. Emily made the connection. "Another attack, doc," said Emily. "We're comin' over right now. Okay? Okay."

"He says okay," said Emily. "He's waiting for us."

The chopper lifted off and headed over to Beaver Island. He landed the chopper and got the captain into the cruiser. McFadden put his driving skills to the test racing over to the doctor. The captain held the rag to his face as McFadden drove wearing only his undies. They had left his pants on the bank; his shirt was saturated with blood and pressed against the captain's face.

"Wow," said Gina. "He didn't even say good-bye."

"He gets a little hyper," said Lisa as she looked around for something to wipe her bloody hands on.

"He'll be back in a jiffy," said Emily. "I hope he doesn't just shove the captain out the door in front of doc's office."

The cruiser's tires squealed as he jammed on the brakes in front of the doc's office. The doc was waiting on the front porch. McFadden ran around to open the door for the captain. Both of the captain's hands were pressing the shirt against his face. He opened the door and helped him out.

"Casual Friday?" asked the doc of McFadden. McFadden looked down at his underwear. He shrugged as he got the captain into the doctor's office. "Gotta run. Gotta go back to North Fox. Here. At least this one's alive," said McFadden.

After dropping off the captain and making sure things were under control, he jumped back in the cruiser and raced back to the airport. McFadden pulled into the airport, hit the brakes, cocked the steering wheel, and did a 180 so the car door was facing the chopper. He jumped out, leaving the keys in the ignition.

"What took you?" chided Gina.

They all jumped into the chopper and lifted off toward the island. In a matter of minutes, they were back at the airstrip. McFadden grabbed some extra rope out of the chopper, then they ran down the dune to where they had left the carp. Once there, McFadden tied a loop onto the end of the rope, threaded it through the gills on one side and started threading the rope through the loop.

"Hold on there, cowboy," said Lisa. "Let me show you how to do that." Lisa untied the loop and tied a much larger loop, then stuck the loop through the carp's mouth and pulled a portion of the loop through each of the gills, then threaded the rope through the loops. This way the fish was supported with the rope through both gills.

"Better. You did better," McFadden admitted. "It does weigh 400 pounds, probably."

"You go get the chopper," said Emily. "Tie two grappling hooks onto the chopper. We'll use the second one to hook the bag. We can take everything at once."

"But I'll have to come back for you."

"No, I'll hook up the fish and jump on for the ride. I'll grab the bag and raft on the way through," she said.

"Whatever. Okay," said McFadden.

"You want to put on some pants, dude?" said Lisa. "There they are."

"Yeah. Might be a good idea," said McFadden.

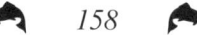

They went up to the chopper. McFadden attached a fifty foot line with a grappling hook to the chopper and another line seventy-five foot long with a grappling hook for the bag. He flew over to the carp and hovered while Emily hooked up the fish and hopped onto the lips of the fish, hanging with one hand onto the rope. McFadden lifted up and flew with the dangling fish, and Emily, below. Emily swung the rope with the other hook and snatched the loop of the rope holding the bag and the raft. They flew to the airport on Beaver Island, lowered the chopper until the fish and the bag touched down and kept lowering until Emily could get off from the fish. She removed the hooks and McFadden flew the chopper fifty feet and set down.

"Okay," said McFadden. "There's your evidence."

CHAPTER SIXTEEN
PREPARING TO DISPLAY THE FISH

Back in town, McFadden stopped over to visit Hank, owner of Hank's Welding. The one welder in town, Hank was always up for an interesting project. "We need to display this fish," he told Hank. "And, we need to do it now. Not tomorrow. I want to hang this fish up this afternoon so it's there tomorrow morning when the town wakes up."

"Six by six inch square steel columns. Welded together. An inverted "U" shape. I-beams welded to the columns for feet. Twenty-eight feet tall. A big hook centered at the top to hang the fish from. No, it doesn't need to be painted. Yes, we will pay for your labor. Yes, you can salvage the steel after the fish is displayed…or wait… maybe we will need it again…Let me think about that."

"Twenty-eight feet tall?" asked Hank. "Twenty-eight feet tall?"

"Yes," said McFadden. "Twenty-eight feet tall."

"So how big is this fish then?"

"It's twenty-four feet, maybe twenty-six. I don't want the tail rubbing on the ground."

"And so," said Hank, "are we just going to throw this rack in your trunk? How are you going to move this?"

"I'm stopping by the shipyard next. The hi-lo they have to move those boats around. They'll be coming to get it. Don't worry about that part. Three hours. I want it done in three hours."

"McFadden, you don't want much, do you? I suppose you'd give me a week to replicate the Eiffel Tower. Very generous of you."

"I'm going to the shipyard now. I'm having the hi-lo here in three hours. Need we waste more time talking about timing or are we on the same page now?"

"Give me four hours."

"Hank, remember the time you smashed your truck into the tree…"

"Oh no, not this again."

"And I didn't include on the report about the drinking…"

"I know," said Hank. He started to mimic McFadden: "I didn't even do a sobriety test…didn't need to…it was obvious…"

McFadden didn't say anything. He just looked straight at Hank.

"Okay then, have it your way McDonald," said Hank.

"McFadden," the officer corrected. "See you in three hours."

McFadden drove over to the shipyard and arranged to have a hi-lo over to Hank's in exactly three hours. "Also, take another one to the airport. Pick up the fish. Take a big pallet. Stick the fish on the pallet, bring back the palletized fish. Bring it to town. We're setting it up in the center of town. Yes, I'm closing down the streets. People can drive around. It's going right in center of town."

"Call me," he said, "when you leave the airport. I'll lead you into town."

McFadden went back to town and started making some calls. First, he called Thomas White, the reporter for the Traverse City Record-Eagle, with affiliation with the local TV station. Everybody called him "Perry."

"Hey Perry—do I ever have the scoop for you. Get your ass over here now. No time for the slow boat. Fly over here now. I'd come and get you but I'm just a little busy. Bring the photog. Bring that hot chick that does the live reporting. Get all the cameras. The dude with the voice boom."

"Yes," said McFadden. "I realize that it's three o'clock. You should be here by five. Yes, plan on spending the night. Yes, I'll arrange the rooms. No, I don't care about your other deadlines. Give those stories about the cat up in the tree to your interns. You want to be here when the fish rolls into town. No, I've never said that before— that's why you need to be here by then."

Next, McFadden called the motel. "I don't know. Five rooms probably. Make it six. Plan on being busy. People are going to be flocking here like Capistranos tomorrow. What? Swallows, whatever, all set? Okay. Gotta run."

He drove over to the local butcher. McFadden barged through the door. "Ice. We are going to need ice. Lots of ice."

"What's the emergency?" asked Frank the butcher.

"We caught a fish!"

"Oh?"

"Look. Don't make me explain. I'm in a rush here. I want two hundred pounds of ice downtown in three hours."

"I can do that."

"Good. I want you there, too. You close at five—no big deal."

"I like to eat at six. Let's make it seven," said Frank.

"Look. Be there at six with the ice and a knife. I'm giving you the honor of slicing open this fish, okay?"

"How big is this fish?"

"Look. I don't have time to explain. What if I told you it was twelve feet long, okay? You with me now? You are going to slice it open, the doc is going to sew it shut, we are going to shove ice down its throat, got it? I'll see you at six—you have a problem with that?"

"I'll be there with bells on," said Frank.

McFadden peeled out and went back to the motel. Emily had taken a shower and was doing a load of laundry. Sitting on the big fish was messier than she had thought.

"Okay girls," said McFadden. "Get your good clothes on. I've got everything arranged."

"McFadden," said Lisa, "I've never seen you so hyper. Maybe driving over to the attack at Indian Point, but other than that, wow, you're wound up!"

"I'm shaking! Look, I got a rack being welded up, a hi-lo moving the fish, another one moving the rack, reporters coming in, the butcher is going to slice that puppy open, doc's going to sew her back up, we're going to shove ice down its throat, and, and…well, isn't that enough?"

"Ah," said Emily, "one problem McFadden. Stomach contents. Can we slice this puppy open before we display the fish?"

"What are you thinking?" he asked.

"I'm thinking that we need to clean her out somewhere before we take her to town."

"Yeah, yeah, yeah," said McFadden. "I see where you're going with this. We're talkin' Betty, right?"

"Might as well get the coroner involved," said Lisa.

"You think Betty's still in there?" asked Gina.

"Where else would she be?" asked Emily. "She is in there…unless we have the wrong fish."

"Poor Betty," said Gina.

"What were you thinking, McFadden…Hang the fish up in front of a crowd and splay her open and all the guts drop out on the street?"

"And Betty?" asked Gina.

"And Betty," said Emily.

"You're going to have more than guts on the street. Trying to create a yak-a-thon?"

"Okay, let's think this through," said McFadden.

"Great idea," said Lisa.

"Poor Betty," said Gina again.

"Okay, look," said McFadden. "You're absolutely right. I'll tell Frank to forget the knife. Let's see. We don't have a lot of time. Think. Think. Think."

Lisa piped in. "You're palletizing the fish, right? Why don't you get another pallet and we'll gut her at the airport. Palletize the guts. Have them waiting for the coroner. He'll appreciate it, I'm sure. He can find Betty."

"Get a big tarp," said Emily. "Maybe put some plywood on the pallet so the tarp doesn't sag between the lathes. Get a tarp and some six mil plastic. Slice her right at the port and wrap up the entrails for the coroner to explore. I'm not sure I'm up for the task, how about you, Lisa?"

"I'd like to gut the fish," said Lisa. "Wouldn't you?"

"Well, yeah," said Emily. "I'm not talking that. I'm just sayin' that I really don't want to pull Betty outta there."

PREPARING TO DISPLAY THE FISH

"It's only been 24 hours...I wonder what condition she'd be in," said Lisa.

"Well," said Emily, "it depends on the size of the pieces. There'd be a lot there...more if she didn't get chewed up too much."

"Poor Betty," said Gina again.

"Did you call the coroner?" asked Lisa.

"No. Didn't think about that yet. Better give him a call now."

"What else might you have forgotten?" asked Lisa.

"Nothing, I don't think I forgot anything else," said McFadden. "Did I?"

"Okay," said Emily, "let's think this through. The welder is welding the rack. The shipyard is moving the rack into town—they can stand it up, right?"

"Yeah. They can stand it," said McFadden.

"Okay," continued Emily. "So we have the rack stood up in town. You get a big pallet, plywood, a tarp, and some plastic and get that over to the airport. The hi-lo is at the airport and lifts the fish up so its guts spill on the pallet. We wrap up the guts for the coroner. Leave them at the airport. The hi-lo puts the fish on another pallet and brings it into town. We shove some ice inside the fish and doc sews him up...hey, how's the captain doing?"

"Haven't heard," said McFadden. "Go on."

"Then the hi-lo lifts the fish up and hangs him from the rack. Then we'll get Lisa up there to shove more ice down its throat."

"Why me? The butcher has the ice. He can shove it down his throat."

"Okay. Frank can do that," said Emily. "Let's see: rack, guts, fish to town, ice, doc, camera crew, reporter. I think we're good."

"Glad we thought about not eviscerating the fish in front of everyone," said Lisa.

"Poor Betty," Gina said.

"Call the coroner," said Emily. "Call him right now."

"Gina, can you run down to the doc's and see how the captain is doing?" asked Lisa. "Tell him what's going on, too. If he is feeling okay, maybe he wants to be in town for the action. He can tell his part of the story."

"Okay," said Gina. "I have one question, though. If you and Emily are gutting this fish at the airport, are you going to change clothes before you appear on camera? If it were me, I'd want to look my best and not have fish guts up to my elbows."

"She might have a point there. We should probably plan on changing," said Lisa. "If we have the chance."

CHAPTER SEVENTEEN
THE MEDIA EVENT

McFadden went to the hardware store and had them deliver the plywood, tarp, and plastic to the airport. "Where do you want it?" they asked.

"Put it by the fish. You'll see it there," he said. Then he added: "Can you take an extension ladder to town for me, 32 footer. I'll need it to hang up the fish."

When the hardware delivered the goods, there were more than fifty people standing around the fish. The word had gotten around the island fast. The one hi-lo had picked up the rack and had stood it up in the center of town. The other machine was at the airport when Emily and Lisa arrived. McFadden shooed the crowd off to the side while the biologists eviscerated the fish. They made sure not to slice through the stomach.

"Look at the heart," said Lisa, "or what little is left of it. The captain shot this puppy right through the center of the heart!"

"Thought the fish went limp quick," said Emily. "The captain knows how to get even."

"Must have been the two tours," laughed Lisa.

The guts spilled out onto the plastic and tarp-covered plywood-reinforced pallet. Betty wasn't visible but undoubtedly was inside the stomach. Emily and Lisa wrapped the plastic over the entrails, then watched as the hi-lo placed the fish on the other pallet. The hi-lo backed up, gently picked up the pallet with the fish on it, and moved toward the gate.

Emily and Lisa hopped in the squad car. McFadden pulled out of the gate first, with his flashers on, followed by the hi-lo and seventeen cars. The hi-lo's top speed was ten MPH, so it was a slow parade to town.

When they arrived, the doc and the captain were there waiting. The captain had a bandage on his face that wrapped all the way around his head. His eyes had blackened. "Well," said Lisa, "how did everything turn out?"

The captain managed a slight smile. "Could have been worse. Could have been worse. The doc says that I'll need a little reconstructive work done in a few weeks after the swelling goes down, but things will turn out okay. How's the fish doing?"

"Well, we just gutted him and I don't know if you knew what you were doing, but you blasted him right in the heart. There wasn't anything left of his heart. Good shot!"

"Yeah, well, I didn't take too much time to aim, really, just blasted him. Instinct. Got that left over from Nam."

"Two tours, right?" asked Lisa as she turned to wink at Emily.

"Yep. Two long, grueling tours."

Emily and Lisa loaded the inside of the fish with twenty bags of ice, then helped hold the sides of the fish together while the doc stitched it up. "Never sutured a fish before," said the doc. "At my age, you'd think there'd be nothing new. Always something new. Last nose I stitched up was sliced by a hunting knife—a guy was making the initial cut in a deer he had hung up and the knife slipped. That was a bad one, too. He cut his nose in half."

The doc continued to stitch up the fish. "This needn't be too pretty, right? Just needs to hold the ice in, right?"

"Yep," said Lisa. "But she'll be on national TV, so do a good job! You don't want people to think you're a hack."

"That's a point. I wonder if they will want to interview me. This could be my fifteen minutes of fame!"

"We'll see. Hey! There's the camera crew now!"

Several people jumped out of a large van that the airport sometimes used to shuttle visitors. A couple of guys had shoulder-mounted cameras and there were two soundmen carrying all sorts of equipment.

Perry came over and approached McFadden. "I thought you said you had a big fish?"

"What?" said McFadden.

"Just kidding. Is this real? This isn't a hoax or something, is it? I'll kill you if this is a hoax."

"Believe me, this puppy is real," answered McFadden. "You're late, you missed the parade. We video-taped it for you. Hey, is that who I think it is?" McFadden pointed over to an area by the van. "Is that Meredith Powers?"

"You got a crush on her or what?" said Perry. "Yep, that's Meredith Powers. You know how you can tell?"

"No."

"See. She's looking in a mirror right now. She's always looking in a mirror. People tune into our station not to hear the news, they want to watch the news."

"I do," admitted McFadden. "Introduce me."

"In a minute. We have to get set up. Now, you're hanging this fish on this rack, I suppose. Let's get a shot of that. Hang on. Let me get these folks organized."

"Don't do anything until we're ready," said Perry to the hi-lo operator.

The doc finished stitching up the fish. Lisa and Emily washed up, McFadden looked at himself in a plate glass storefront window and combed his hair. Gina checked her hair and nails. The doc went over to a car's side view mirror and looked himself over. He smiled in the mirror, making sure he didn't have anything stuck between his teeth. He had always been self-conscious about that. The doc then went over to a hose bibb and washed his arms up to his elbows. Everybody was ready.

Meredith came over, looking beautiful, and gauged the lighting. "I'll be standing over here, with the fish behind me. Make sure that the lighting always shines on the left side of my face. This is hard for me to admit, but this morning I woke up with a little zit on the right side of my chin. I hate it when that happens!"

"You look beautiful, Meredith. I can't even see anything," said Perry. "Okay boys, let's get ready to roll."

The director repositioned the cameras slightly. "We are ready...3, 2, 1, ACTION."

"Good evening everyone, Meredith Powers for Action Eight News. Well, you've all heard of fish stories before and the big one that got away. Well, I must say I thought someone was pulling my leg," she said, looking down at her beautiful gams, then winking at the camera, "but this is a fish story that is true, and we have the proof."

"Pan to the fish, you idiot, not her legs! Pan to the fish," the director told the cameraman.

"This fish was choppered in from North Fox Island, brought to the airstrip here on Beaver Island, then carried to town with this backhoe."

"Pan to the loader. Pan to the loader. It's a hi-lo, Meredith."

"It's a hi-lo, Meredith, the director is saying. What I'm saying is that this is quite the fish. They are going to hang this fish up on the rack behind me so that we can get a really good look at it. Okay, I think we're ready to hang the fish."

The hi-lo lifted up the fish. McFadden was on the ladder resting against the rack. He slipped the noose of the rope around the hook on the rack, then the hi-lo began to lower the fish. McFadden got down from the ladder and Frank, right on cue, took several bags of ice up and started shoving them down the fish's throat.

Meredith continued: "Officer McCracken just slipped the noose over the hook, now the hi-lo is lowering gently. This is a delicate procedure. You wouldn't want to drop a fish like this! Have a correction: It's Officer McFadden that was slipping the noose over the hook. Now they're shoving ice down its throat."

"Let's see if we can get some information from the officer: Officer McFadden...I have your name right now, don't I, okay, sorry about the mistake before...Now, tell us about this monster!"

"We take our work seriously here on Beaver Island, protecting the safety of every resident and visitor who comes not only to this island, but also to neighboring islands. We had a report that several people were missing on neighboring North Fox Island and an eyewitness reported seeing her friend being, ah, attacked by a large fish. At my request, two biologists and the coast guard, as well as a revered captain of the coast guard came over to assist with our search. We hunted down this fish and are confident that this is the fish that attacked and killed a young college student. Her name is being withheld until positive identification is made and her next of kin are notified."

"My. You are the type of officer every community should have. Now, how did you find and capture this fish?"

"Let me turn this over to the captain. As you will see, the protection of the public often comes with a cost."

"Captain Jack Summers...come over here...it looks as though you've had better days. What went on here?" asked Meredith.

"Well, I flew in the two biologists and offered to stay and help with this recovery operation. We combed the confirmed areas and addressed the crime scene where the fish attack took place. We discovered the location where the fish was hiding out. I was trying to extract the fish when it came up and tried to take my head off. I reared backward to get out of the way but it still caught my nose, removing a portion of it. I'd show you the damage, but it's not too pleasant."

"That's okay captain, we can see how serious it must be. What happened next?"

"I had a loaded shotgun with me. I spun it around and shot the puppy right through the heart, killing it instantly."

"Oh my, captain, that must have been frightening. Weren't you scared?"

"No. I operate on instinct. Veteran of Nam. Did two tours. Two long grueling tours."

"Well, I know that I speak for all of us when I say thank you for your service and for the sacrifice we see you made here today. Without people like you, America would not be the great country it is. Thank you again. Now where are those biologists you mentioned?"

Lisa and Emily went over to Meredith. "Lisa Brown. Emily French, I have your names right? Okay, didn't want to mess up another name. One mistake a day is all I allow myself," she said, winking at the camera. "What do you make of all of this?"

Lisa went first: "We have studied these invasive Asian Carp, Emily and I have, for many years. We started studying them back before they even got into Lake

Michigan. We inhibited their spread but eventually they worked their way into Lake Michigan. They have been evolving, they are very dangerous, and they have changed the ecosystem. Emily."

"We have worked with the Shedd Aquarium in Chicago, as well as with the Corps of Engineers, the coast guard and the Department of Natural Resources. Even with all of these agencies involved, and with drastic measures being taken, such as the electrified grids in the Chicago River, this invasive species has made its way into Lake Michigan. We are not alarmists, but believe that it is only a matter of time—and a very short time by the way—that these fish will migrate into the other four Great Lakes. We believe that they will continue to increase in size, will continue to evolve, and will continue to take human life."

Lisa jumped in. "This fish is 24 feet long. This may not be the largest fish out there. Undoubtedly, there are larger ones. We need to inform the public, too, not only is the water unsafe, the last three attacks happened on land. Walking down the beach is hazardous. These fish are beginning to conquer land. Be aware of this and stay out of the water and away from the water's edge. For all we know, they may be migrating inland a greater distance than what we now have documented. It will only get worse."

"Do you have anything to add, Emily," asked Meredith.

"When foreign species are introduced into our environment—these carp were imported from Asia—catastrophic things often occur. Dutch Elm Beetles killed the Elm trees in America, Emerald Ash Borers killed the Ash trees in America, Zebra Mussels and Quagga Mussels have altered the food chain in the Great

Lakes, anacondas are changing the ecosystem in the Everglades and I could go on and on. Who would ever think that we would have anacondas slithering around America? Who would think that we would have carp the size of sharks eating people in Lake Michigan? I'm only 30, and this has all happened within my lifetime!"

Lisa piped in: "There are no easy answers. If there were, we'd tell you right now what they are. Support the environment and be careful on how you alter it. For now, be wary about being anywhere around the water. To emphasize this: within the stomach contents of this fish was a young female college student."

"Officer McFadden, would you like to add something as well?"

"I would first like to thank the doctor over there for all his help." Doc gave a big smile for the camera and waved. "As a protector of the public safety, I would like to emphasize what was just said. The water and the beach in and around Lake Michigan are unsafe. We do not need to have more tragedies. Until we have more information, I cannot confirm this, but we believe that there have been seven deaths associated with these carp. Please be careful!"

"Okay," said Meredith. "We shall consider ourselves forewarned. More on this tonight at 11. This is Meredith Powers for Channel 8 out of Traverse City, Michigan with this breaking story. We are the first to report this story. National news stations have been contacting us and we will be sharing this tremendous story with them tonight, and remember: You heard it first, right here, on Channel 8. Meredith Powers, reporting."

LAKESHARK! INVASION OF THE ASIAN CARP

CHAPTER EIGHTEEN
THE CORONER

Later that evening, the coroner came over to go through the stomach contents of the fish. Lisa, Emily, McFadden, and Gina all went to the airport to watch the developments. "Well," he said, "business is picking up."

"Yes it is," said McFadden.

"Now then, usually the bodies get brought to me. I normally don't have to extract them. However, in this case I see why you may want to have me do this. Let's see. I'll make a cut here, wow, the stomach sure is full. Hummm…here's the girl. Well preserved. A couple of fish—you're not interested in those are you?"

"Well," said Emily, "actually since we have the contents there, Lisa and I would like to go through it a bit."

"Oh yeah," said Lisa. "Sure we would."

"Okay then, here's Betty!"

The coroner pulled Betty out of the stomach as if he were delivering a baby. She had been eaten whole. Still recognizable, one could tell that she was a beautiful girl.

"Betty!" said Gina. "Oh, Betty."

"She'll clean up well," said the coroner. "Open casket if her folks want. Will need a little make-up. We have a gal that does the hair—beautiful job. Loves her work. Says her hairdos last an eternity. They do."

"What else do we have in there?" questioned Emily.

"Well, let's take a look. I'll put Betty aside here for a moment. Hummmm. Well, this looks like a small carp, another small carp. Oh! Here's a perch. Don't see those too much anymore. Nice sized one, too. Hey!!! Another perch…nice! Maybe they're coming back. A carp, carp, tiny carps, here a carp, there a carp. Hungry guy. That's about it. Oh, well, looky here. Here's a hand. Looks male. Well-groomed nails."

"Probably Joe," Gina said. "Those other guys didn't take very good care of their nails. You think this carp picked it up after another one ate him?"

"I'd say," said the coroner. "Nobody else here."

"What do you do with the hand?" asked Gina.

"I'll send it to the forensic lab. They'll run the prints for an ID. It's always good to have a positive ID. Takes the worry away from the families. Otherwise they hold out false hope. Better to have closure."

"Can I see it?" asked Gina.

"Sure. It's right here. Suit yourself."

"Hummm…that's Joe. He had sort of big fingers like that. Hi Joe!" said Gina.

"You're taking this pretty well," said McFadden. "I'm a bit surprised."

"Well," said Gina, "I never thought I'd be interested in this stuff but it is fascinating. You know, I sort of thought I wanted to teach kindergarten, but I never really liked kids that much. Maybe I could go into police work, or forensics. People always teased me about not having any brains, but I think I just sort of played it down some. Maybe I liked the attention a bit. I'm not really such a dingbat."

"I never thought of you as a dingbat," said McFadden.

"Really?" said Gina.

"I just thought you were so beautiful when I first saw you—you were wearing that old shirt and not much else—what wasn't there to like?"

"Well," said Gina, "I have an admission to make. That cute shark underwear you had on was a complete turn-on. Remember I called you a hottie!"

"You said sort of a hottie."

"I corrected myself. I didn't want to appear forward."

The coroner pulled his arm out of the stomach. "You guys. Just kiss each other and get it over with!"

"Good idea," said Emily. "You're turning us on!"

Gina made the first move and wrapped her arms around McFadden. She gave McFadden a big kiss. "You know," she said, "I believe I heard the motel owner say she needed my room tonight. Any place you know of that I could stay?"

McFadden blushed. "Well, usually when I find a place for someone to stay it's in the jail cell."

"Sexxxxy!" said Gina.

"But I think I can do better than that."

"Say McFadden," said Emily. "Lisa and I are going to stick around tonight and then blast off tomorrow, so maybe we can all have breakfast in the morning so we can say good-bye."

"That's good. Sure do appreciate the help," he said.

"You want to join us, Mr. Coroner?" asked Lisa.

"Well, perhaps so. Probably should wash up a bit before that, though."

"I guess we're all going to need a good hot shower," said Lisa. "Except for Gina. She might need a cold one!"

"Speaking of cold ones, let's hit the bar," said Emily. "I need to talk to you about something, Lisa."

CHAPTER NINETEEN
MAKING ARRANGEMENTS

Everybody left the airport. McFadden made arrangements for the entrails to be picked up and disposed of. The coroner took Betty and the hand over to the Beaver Islander boat and placed them on ice. He would take the boat back to mainland tomorrow. McFadden dropped Gina off at her hotel so she could take a cold shower and check out. McFadden then went over to the hanging carp to check out the crowd. Most of the islanders were there—it was the most exciting thing to happen on Beaver Island since the assassination of James Strang, a cult leader killed by his followers back in 1856.

Emily and Lisa went to the bar. They ordered a pitcher. "You know," said Emily, "I think our work is done here."

"Yeah," said Lisa, "I wonder if the captain will feel good enough to fly us out in the morning."

"No," said Emily. "I mean our work is done."

"What?"

"Our work. We studied carp, we did everything we could. We couldn't stop them. We tried. The genie is out of the lamp. The toothpaste is out of the tube. The can of worms has been opened. You know what I mean?"

"No. What do you mean?"

"I mean, it's time to do something else," said Emily.

Lisa got a worried look on her face. "You want to split up?"

"Lisa! NO! No, no, no. Never."

"Well, what then?"

"You know how we mentioned anacondas on the news today? Let's go down to the Everglades and study the snakes. I've about had it with carp."

"Really. The Everglades. Maybe we could save the Everglades," said Lisa.

"That's what I'm thinking. Change of pace, too. Maybe take a little time off. Milk our fifteen minutes of fame. Go on CNN, The Tonight Show, how about Good Morning America!"

"Okay."

"We can wear our field outfits. Look the part."

"Maybe write a story," said Emily. "It would make a good story."

CHAPTER TWENTY
WRAPPING THINGS UP

Captain Jack and the coroner arrived early for breakfast. They secured a table by the window.

"Look," said the captain as he motioned his hand toward the window. "There's McFadden."

"Is that Gina?" asked the coroner.

"Oh my."

McFadden and Gina walked into the restaurant. Gina's hair was cropped to above her shoulders.

"Almost didn't recognize you," said the coroner.

"I had McFadden give me a quick cut this morning," said Gina. "He's multi-talented!"

"Looks good," said the captain. "There's something else…what is it?"

"Trimmed my nails. Broke two pulling that carp out of the burrow. Decided I didn't need long nails anyways. I've been doing some thinking."

Everybody seemed to have new plans. McFadden had just found out that morning that Gina was changing her major to Criminal Justice and was going to study up at Northern in the UP. If everything worked out, he was going to find a position for her on the island. Gina had fallen in love—not just with McFadden but also with the island. She liked the friendly people and how you could leave your keys in the car ignition.

McFadden admitted that his "bad ass" nature was only a cover-up for loneliness. Really, he admitted, he was a sensitive guy. He was ready to settle down. Gina was the woman of his dreams. From the minute he saw her wearing that white, ill-fitting man's shirt, and little else, he knew he was in love.

Gina sheepishly admitted that she really partied more than she wanted to, just trying to keep up with her now deceased buddies. She was done with being dumb Gina, she was done with playing with her hair, she was done with doing her nails. She was ready to commit to getting through school.

McFadden said that he felt that he could not live without her, and that he would take the chopper up to Northern every weekend to see her, even though it would leave the island without police assistance. "That will show them that they need a deputy here," he said. "Sometimes she can fly in, or take the boat. One way or another, we are going to make it work out." Lisa nudged Emily. She pointed out that the lovebirds were holding hands beneath the table.

The coroner had new plans, too. Taking Betty out of the carp's stomach made him yearn for the days back in medical school when he delivered babies. He decided to expand his practice to help out mid-wives. "That way," he said, "I'm working both angles."

The captain, with his close call with death, had made serious life decisions as well. "I called the VA. I volunteered. There's such a problem with PTSD. The poor guys coming back from battle. They're more screwed up than I am. I can help, and they can help me. I know what it's like. I think I can help them improve. And, I really think that I can improve. I'm tired of thinking about Vietnam."

"Say Captain," said Gina as she reached down inside her swimsuit top. "Sorry for the informality, but I don't even have a purse here." She pulled out a newly-minted $100. The bill had never been folded. "Thanks for spotting me the cash so I could buy some clothes."

The captain took the bill and looked at it closely. "Maybe I'll just hang onto this for good luck."

And then there's Emily and Lisa. Well, they had cemented their plans together. They had made some calls. The Shedd Aquarium was willing to sponsor them on their new quest. They would head down to Florida in a week. They would study the anacondas and whatever else was harming the ecosystem down in the 'Glades.

The Shedd was sending for the carp, too. It would be stuffed and hung from the ceiling in the foyer of the Shedd. It would be a reminder of what could happen if things got out of control. They would have a naming contest for it. The carp would be famous.

Doc came walking into the restaurant. "How's the nose, captain?"

"Still on," he said. "I think you did a nice job."

"Well good. It might be one of the last ones I do. I've decided to take a bit of a break. I called my grandkids. Going down to visit them for a while. With all the action around here, I decided I was missing out on some of the things I should be paying attention to. By the way, nice haircut, Gina." Gina smiled at the doc. "I've lined up a younger friend of mine to come and take over."

"Really!" said McFadden. "Well, I think that's a great idea. Say, did you hear about the carp?"

"What's that?" asked the doc.

"The Shedd Aquarium is going to pick it up and have it stuffed. Good thing you did such a nice job stitching it up. They are going to hang it from the ceiling, so the cut is what people are going to see."

"I mean, I know they will have to open her back up, but no damage was done. Your suturing will be on display for all to see. Take your grandchildren over there to see it. It will be as famous as Sue the dinosaur at the Field Museum in Chicago."

"Maybe more famous," said the doc. "Good to hear."

"They want you at the unveiling, too."

"I'll be. I never thought an island doc would get all this attention."

"They said that they saw you on the news. Said your smile stole the spotlight from Meredith Powers!"

"Oh, I'm not sure about that," said the doc.

"Well," said McFadden, "I guess that wraps it up. Let's all stay in touch. Lisa, Emily: now don't you go down to the Everglades and find an eighty foot long anaconda."

"You just never know what's going to happen," said Emily. "What do you think, Lisa?"

Lisa pondered the question for a moment. "Anything's possible."

LAKESHARK! INVASION OF THE ASIAN CARP

LAKESHARK! INVASION OF THE ASIAN CARP